The Old West

VAN HOLT

BUCK HAYDEN, MUSTANGER

Ride the Old West

Cover and Book design: KB Graphix & Design • www.kbdesign1.com

First Printing, 2014. Printed in the United States of America.

CHAPTER 1

Hayden was surprised when he saw smoke curling from the rock chimney. He had figured the old shack below the mesa wall would still be empty. No one had lived there in years. The desert stretching away to the east was too dry and barren for raising anything but rocks, and they grew by themselves. It was no better up on the mesa.

He was even more surprised when he saw the woman standing at the shack door, watching him approach.

When he rode into the dusty yard and drew rein he saw that she was still in her twenties, though at first glance she looked older. Her face was tired and drawn. Her eyes were faded and faint wrinkles and already begun to appear around them. She was tall and slender but rather well developed in all the right places—even her shapeless cotton dress could not hide that fact.

When he touched his flat-crowned black hat, she responded with a slight nod and said, "My husband went to town for supplies, but you're welcome to water your horse and eat here. I'll soon have a bite ready."

"Thanks," he said, stepping down from the saddle. "I'll take the water but pass up the grub. I need to push on."

She silently watched him fill his canteen and water his horse at the half-rotted plank trough. She knew he was wondering about her being here in the old shack, but he asked no questions and hid his curiosity behind a weather-beaten face that was expressionless except for just a hint of wry humor around the thin lips. His eyes were blue but did not seem to have much color until he looked directly at her. Then for a moment the color deepened to a clear sky blue, the change apparently caused by a kind of instinctive alertness. They were not cold eyes, just utterly devoid of warmth.

He seemed a tough, quiet, lonely man, a little remote and unapproachable because he needed no one and preferred to mind his own business. There was no sign of weakness in him, and certainly no softness. He was lean and hard, standing over six feet tall and weighing around a hundred and eighty pounds. He wore a dusty black suit that fit him well, and two guns, one in a cross-draw holster on the left. Both holsters were tied down.

"Do you need two guns?" she asked.

He glanced at her with that brief intensity in his eyes that she had noticed before. A faint, wry smile touched his hard mouth. "They come in handy now and then."

Even as he spoke he looked away, and following his glance, she saw the riders approaching.

Deliberately, he checked his long-barreled revolvers, drawing one at a time, then stood silently watching the riders.

"Do you expect trouble?" she asked uneasily.

He remained standing near his red horse and did not look around at her. He kept his attention on the four riders. "In this country," he said, "it always pays to expect trouble. Speaking for myself, I'm hardly ever disappointed."

"Are you from around here?" she asked.

"I come and go."

The four riders were all young men in their twenties. They made a show of riding boldly into the yard and pulling up in a cloud of dust. Their reckless eyes shifted from Hayden to the woman and back again.

The one in the green shirt said with a sneer, "Well, if it ain't the big bad Buck Hayden himself. What the hell are you doin' here?"

Hayden moved his broad shoulders in a brief shrug. "Passing by."

"Well, you better keep passin'," the rider said, and then turned his eyes on the woman at the door. "Where's your old man?"

"He went to town." Her eyes were uneasy and after a moment she added, "He should be back soon."

"Not unless he left yesterday," the same one snickered, pushing his narrow-brimmed hat back on his curly head. "It'll take him all day in that old wagon. Anyway, it don't matter. You can tell him for us. He better pack up and clear out. This is the last warnin'. He's squattin' on Crown range."

"Since when?" Hayden asked.

The curly head turned back toward him. "Since I said it was," he sneered. "You want to make something of it?"

"Take it easy, Skip," one of the others muttered, watching Hayden with worried eyes.

"Shut up, Pete!" Skip snarled. "Don't nobody tell Skip Leggett what to do!"

"Just Hoffer," Pete grumbled. "And he told us not to cause no trouble where it wasn't necessary."

"What does Hoffer want with this place?" Hayden asked. "Ain't everything west of the mesa enough for him?"

"I reckon he'll be the one to decide that," Skip retorted. He seemed unable to speak in a civil tone. Every word he spoke sounded like a threat or a challenge.

Hayden glanced at the other three. Pete Grimes still seemed anxious to avoid trouble, but Tony Bick and Cal Whitty were grinning maliciously, as if they were enjoying themselves. Hayden considered Tony Bick the most dangerous one of the four. Bick was a tall slender young man with laughing blue eyes and big white teeth. He let Skip Leggett do the talking because that was what Skip was good at, but Bick was ready to do the shooting if there was trouble.

Hayden noticed that Cal Whitty was wearing an extra gun that looked familiar, but he thought it unlikely that it was the one he had in mind. The bottom of Whitty's coat hid both shell belts, and a straggly mustache hid part of his grin.

Hayden's pale eyes turned a shade colder. "You boys better drift along," he said.

Skip Leggett's right hand tensed like a claw over the butt of his holstered gun. His handsome face turned ugly with sneering anger. "Who says?"

Hayden looked deliberately at that threatening hand. "I say," he said quietly.

Pete Grimes spoke quickly. "Remember what Hoffer said, Skip. He said he'd have our hides if we overstepped his orders."

Skip Leggett slowly relaxed and let out the breath he had been holding. His expression remained a sneer, his voice remained sarcastic. "Well, it don't matter whether I kill you now or later, Hayden. But if I wait till Hoffer tells me to do it, he might even give me a bonus."

"You'll earn it," Hayden told him in the same quiet tone.

Skip glared murder at him but said nothing. Pete Grimes looked relieved, Tony Bick and Cal Whitty disappointed. Skip seemed disgusted because his instructions from Hoffer denied him the pleasure of killing Hayden.

He turned his scornful eyes to the woman. "Tell your old man we'll be back, but the next time we'll come shootin'."

She remained silent, hugging herself against the cold wind that the others seemed unaware of. Dust and tumbleweeds drifted across the bleak gray Nevada desert. One tumbleweed rolled up against the water trough and crouched there shivering. The tall man called Hayden stood motionless in the yard, his face like stone, his cold pale eyes never leaving the Crown riders.

Skip Leggett reined his horse around, watching Hayden over his shoulder. "You're the one who better drift along, Hayden," he said. "You better drift right on out of the country. The next time I see you, I'm bettin' I'll have orders from Hoffer to kill you."

"You better bring plenty of help."

Leggett snorted at that and put his horse into a furious gallop back the way they had come. The others were close behind him. Tony Bick threw a look of mock terror back at Hayden, flashing and blinking his eyes wildly. Cal Whitty bent over in his saddle laughing.

"Who is this Hoffer who keep sending men over here?" the woman asked.

Hayden's attention was still on the Crown riders as they followed the dusty trail around a rocky projection of the mesa wall, and he did not answer until they were out of sight. Then a cold smile twisted his lips and he said, "King Hoffer. He came here from Texas a couple years back and pretty soon the people who were already here found out they were squatting on his range. I don't guess they liked it much, but so far nobody's done anything about it. He's either bought out or scared out nearly everyone in the whole country."

"Have you got a place around here?" she asked.

"Not me," he said, stepping into the saddle, all his movements unhurried and effortless. "When I'm around here I stay with Frank Martin and help him hunt wild horses to earn my keep." He smiled faintly. "We used to do that in West Texas before he came here."

The woman looked at him in surprise. "Haven't you heard? He was killed about a week ago. My husband heard about it in town.

Some of Hoffer's men went to his place and he tried to run them off with a shotgun, and one of them killed him. That's the story they've been telling anyway."

Hayden's face seemed to turn to stone and a bleak empty look came into his eyes. "When they turned to leave, I thought that was Frank's shotgun and scabbard on Skip Leggett's saddle, and if I'm not mistaken Cal Whitty had his old Starr pistol."

CHAPTER 2

After leaving the shack, Hayden rode north for a half mile along the trail that wound along the foot of the mesa, then put his horse up a steep side trail that climbed the mesa wall. Before he left, the woman had said her name was Helen Mead and her husband was Carl Mead, who had come west for his health. Seeing the look in Hayden's eyes, she had told him to be careful, and he had told her to watch out for Hoffer's men, for they would be back.

The tracks of Skip Leggett and the others kept going north toward town, but Hayden swung west across the windswept mesa, ten miles of rocks and stunted gray brush and bleached grass and not much else—ten miles across, closer to twenty from north to south. The Martin shack, which Hayden reached in late afternoon, was near the center of the mesa.

The place was deserted. The shack door stood open, creaking in the wind. The pole corrals were empty, the horses gone. There was a fresh grave near the house. At least they had buried Frank.

Hayden dismounted and stood gazing at the grave with bleak eyes. Frank Martin had been the only man he had thought of as a friend in a long time, and this old shack on the mesa was the only place left that he had thought of as home, the place he always came back to. It would not be the same without Frank. Nothing would be the same without Frank. He and Hayden had been like brothers, and were in fact stepbrothers.

After a time Hayden entered the shack. They had strewn Frank's clothes and all his things on the floor, apparently looking for money. Even his black suit lay on the floor gathering dust with everything else.

It was then that Hayden first became aware of the cold rage building inside him. He had bought the suit for Frank in Virginia City when he had bought the one he himself was wearing and had given it to him the last time he was here. They were almost exactly the same size, so whatever fit one fit the other. Frank had been so proud of his new suit that he would not wear it, saying he was saving it for his wedding or his funeral, whichever came first. He had not known any women well enough to think of marriage, so he must have known it would be his funeral.

But he had been buried in the old clothes he was wearing when he was murdered, and Hayden was sure that they had not built him a coffin. Murderers did not build coffins for their victims. The surprise was that they had buried him at all. They must have received orders from Hoffer to do so. The cattle king probably wanted no dead men lying around on what he considered his range.

Hayden stared at an empty coffee can on the floor. So they had found the money, he thought. It had been Hayden's money, not Frank Martin's. Yet this did not anger him as did the sight of Frank's new suit lying wrinkled and dusty on the floor.

The shack door slammed and suddenly there was a cocked gun in Hayden's hand. But he realized it was the wind that had caused the door to bang and he slid the long lean dark revolver back into the holster.

Frank's guns were gone. Hayden had been right in thinking that Skip Leggett had Martin's shotgun and Cal Whitty had his pistol. They were so sure nothing would be done about Frank's death that they did not care who saw them with his guns.

Hayden took a deep breath and let it out slowly. Then for a time he stood listening to the sound of the wind moaning outside the shack. The wind blew dust in through the cracks between the warped gray boards of the walls. It was turning colder, and the light was already fading. He needed a few things from town, but he and his horse were both tired from travel. He decided to stay here tonight and head for town early in the morning.

Going outside, he stripped the gear from the bay, rubbed him down good and let him drink at the waterhole near the shack, then turned him loose to graze. The gelding would not stray far—not unless he was driven off. Hayden returned to the shack thinking about Frank's horses, wondering if any of them might still be around. Most of them had been mustangs that Frank was breaking to the saddle and getting ready to sell, but there had been a buckskin and a roan, both geldings, that he had not wanted to part with.

Hoffer's men had not taken Frank's grub, at least not all of it, and there was a stack of dry wood in the corner near the rock fireplace. Hayden built a fire, boiled a pot of coffee and cooked pan bread, a can of beans and several thick slices of bacon for his supper. While he ate he thought about Helen Mead, wondering if her husband had returned from town or if she was still alone in the old shack below the mesa wall.

Then his thoughts strayed to Rose Hoffer and a sigh escaped his lips. He had seen her only a few times, had never spoken to her at all, but seeing her only once would have been enough for him to know he would never forget her. He had been a lot of places and seen a lot of women, but he had never seen another like Rose Hoffer.

But she was King Hoffer's daughter and that put her beyond Hayden's reach, now more than ever. She was unaware of his existence, but before long she would hate him.

After supper he cleaned his guns, his long-barreled Colts and his Winchester, by the dying firelight, then went outside for a careful look around before turning in. The bay was grazing not far away and raised his head to look at him. Hayden smiled faintly in the dark. That horse was the only friend he had left, now that Frank was dead.

A raw cold wind was blowing dust across the mesa the next morning when he set out for town. He turned up the collar of his sheepskin coat. Under the coat he wore a blue double-breasted shirt, and gray wool trousers. His black suit was in his blanket roll behind the saddle. He could have left it at the shack, but he doubted if anything would be safe there. Not for long, anyway.

As he rode he watched the barren gray ridges for any sign of Hoffer's men or the horses they had driven off. He had considered the possibility that they might not have driven them far, intending to return for them when a buyer turned up or they had a chance to drive them to one. It was even possible that Hoffer himself did not know they had driven off the horses or stolen the money that had been in the tin can.

At the north rim of the mesa Hayden halted to study the country below. He sat there for a time on his red horse, his pale eyes searching the hazy distance for riders but seeing none. Then he put the bay down the steep rocky slope and rode on toward town, arriving there about midmorning.

A grim smile twisted his lips when he saw the man up on a ladder painting Hoffer's name in large letters on the sign at the edge of town. He drew rein and said, "Looks like the town has got itself a new name."

The man turned a red face and gave him a mean look, then went on painting. "Hoffer's orders."

Hayden recalled seeing the man around the general store, loading supplies in wagons and doing odd jobs around the place. A sort of general flunky with important airs. "You working for Hoffer now?" Hayden asked.

"Looks that way," the man grunted. "He bought out a half interest in the store and now Mr. Boyle jumps when Hoffer says jump. He's been runnin' around like a chicken with its head cut off and yellin' at me about ever'thing, afraid Hoffer will come in and complain about somethin'."

Hayden smiled faintly. "Well, I imagine a man like you needs two bosses to keep you in line."

The man snorted but said nothing, and Hayden walked his horse on down the town's only street. He noticed that Hoffer's name had already been painted on the general store—above Boyle's name. *Hoffer & Boyle, General Mdse.*

Boyle appeared at the door in a dirty apron, a wild look in his eyes and a pinched look around his mouth, and yelled, "Hurry up with that, Stacy! I've got some work for you to do in the store!"

"I'm working just as fast as I can," Stacy replied.

Hayden drew rein and shifted his weight in the saddle, grinning at the sign on the store. Then he glanced along the street, which was deserted except for a wagon standing in front of the restaurant. "Has everybody in town sold out to Hoffer, or just you?"

Boyle's mouth fell open and he blinked at Hayden as though wondering where he had seen him before. Hayden had only been in the store a time or two. "Mr. Hoffer's my new partner, if that's what you mean. But I'm still running the store, like always."

"He wouldn't happen to be in town, would he?" Hayden asked.

"No, he's out at his ranch, as far as I know." Boyle stared at

Hayden in silence for a moment. The storekeeper had thinning sandy hair, a small sharp nose, and practically no chin. "Now I remember you. You're that mustanger who came here a time or two with Frank Martin."

"Frank was the mustanger. I just helped him out when I was around."

Boyle's eyes strayed toward the sign Stacy was painting a short distance away at the edge of the small town. "I knew I hadn't seen you around here much, and Martin only came in when he needed supplies. Never had much to say."

"He didn't owe you anything, did he?"

"No, and I'm glad of it," Boyle said. "Mr. Hoffer said not to give anyone credit without his okay."

Hayden's wry smile returned. "I thought you were still running the store."

Boyle's face got red and he looked at Hayden with resentment in his small sharp eyes. "I am, but him being my partner and all, naturally I'd want to talk to him before giving anyone credit."

Hayden's smile remained, but there was no warmth in it. "Naturally."

Boyle looked him over deliberately, looking for something that would make Boyle himself feel superior. But there was very little about Hayden that would make a man like Boyle feel superior. Instead, what he saw filled him with envy. Hayden looked big and strong and tough, and with his dark hair, pale blue eyes and lean bronzed face he was a strikingly handsome man. Nor was there anything about his clothes or his saddle to look down on, and even Boyle, who knew nothing about horses, could tell that the blood bay was a better horse than the average cowhand rode.

Yet Hayden had as good as admitted being a drifter, a man who shunned steady work, and that made Boyle wonder how he could afford such an animal. Looking at the tied-down guns, Boyle suspected that he made his living with them. He might even be an outlaw.

"Besides," Boyle added, pretending that he was still talking about Martin although it was Hayden he actually had in mind, "I didn't know him well enough to trust him. Never gave anybody around here a chance to get acquainted with him. And he had a sort of a mean look in his eyes. I figured a man like that would get himself killed sooner or later."

Hayden's smile faded and his eyes turned cold. He stared at Boyle a moment in silence, and then said, "I've known Frank Martin all my life. He hated trouble. That was the reason he kept to himself. He said the only way to avoid trouble was to stay away from people."

"Well, that's not what I heard," Boyle said. "Mr. Hoffer sent those boys up there to see him about buying his claim, and he tried to run them off with a shotgun."

"I imagine it was the other way around," Hayden said. "I imagine they tried to run him off. They've already run just about everybody else out of the country." He glanced at the sign on the store. "Or forced them to sell."

"They never forced me to sell," Boyle said. "Times have been so hard I was afraid I might have to close the store, especially with so many people moving away. But Mr. Hoffer assured me that wouldn't happen if I went in with him."

"Don't think he's doing it for nothing. My guess is he just wanted a place to get his supplies wholesale. With him owning part of the store, you won't make anything on what he buys for himself. And when his hands trade here, he'll get back some of the wages he pays them, so he'll win both ways. You'll be the big loser in the long run."

A bitter look came into Boyle's eyes. "Well, I didn't have much choice. He said if I didn't take his offer, he'd open a store of his own and drive me out of business."

Hayden nodded. "I figured something like that." A gust of cold wind tugged at his hat and he squinted his eyes against the blowing dust, turning his attention to the wagon across the street. "Do you know whose wagon that is?"

"Belongs to that squatter who moved into that old shack below the mesa," Boyle said. "He got supplies here earlier, then stopped over there. He seems to spend a lot of time at the restaurant."

Hayden thought of Helen Mead, who had no doubt spent the night alone in the old shack, worrying about her husband and wondering if Hoffer's men would return before he got back. It must have been a very long night for her.

Frowning, Hayden reined his horse across the street, tied him to the rail near the wagon and entered the restaurant. The picture he had formed in his mind of Carl Mead was that of a pale, sickly looking man, thin and stoop-shouldered. But the man he saw sitting on the stool at the counter looked to him like the picture of health. Mead was close to six feet tall, had a good set of shoulders and a strong jaw darkened by a day-old stubble. The only indication of imperfect health was that he coughed when he turned his head to watch Hayden come through the door, and Hayden had observed that a lot of people coughed when there was nothing wrong with them.

A pretty red-haired girl stood behind the counter, and it was obvious that she and Mead had been talking. There was no one else in the place. Hayden glanced at the girl, then frowned at Mead.

"You Carl Mead?"

Mead silently nodded, watching him with frank curiosity in his brown eyes. He was wearing a new tan stetson that was pushed back on wavy dark hair and a corduroy coat. He did not appear to be armed.

Hayden thumbed his own hat back off his frowning forehead and said, "I stopped by your place yesterday to water my horse and some of Hoffer's men showed up while I was there. They were looking for you and they said they'd be back. I imagine your wife's worried sick by now."

There was only a trace of worry on Mead's too handsome face as he asked, "They didn't bother her, did they?"

"No, but they weren't very polite." A wry, humorless smile twisted Hayden's lips. "If I wasn't such a peace-loving fellow, I might have taught them some manners."

"I guess I better get back out there," Mead said. But he seemed reluctant to leave his stool at the counter. He glanced down at his empty plate, finished his coffee and laid some money on the counter as he rose. He looked silently at the red-haired girl and she looked back at him with a slight frown in her hazel eyes, as if she expected some word or gesture from him that she knew he would not give her in front of Hayden. Mead only touched his hat, said, "Thanks," and went out past Hayden, turning up the collar of his coat against the cold wind.

Hayden glanced at the girl, then turned to follow Mead outside. "You ain't quite what I expected," he said.

Mead looked around at him. "How do you mean?"

"Your wife said you came out here because of your health," Hayden said with a twisted grin. "I expected you to look a little more sickly."

Mead put his hands over his mouth and coughed violently. "It's my lungs."

Hayden looked at him with worried eyes. "That ain't catching, is it?"

Before Mead could answer, a shout drew their attention to two riders just entering town.

"Well, look what we got here!" Skip Leggett jeered, leaning forward in his saddle and staring at them as if he could not believe his eyes. He reined in and said, "It looks like our luck's finally changin', Cal. We done found Hayden and that squatter at the same time. We can kill two birds with one stone. Or should I say, two chickens with one bullet?"

Cal Whitty grinned but said nothing. He was still wearing Frank Martin's pistol reversed on his left hip.

Carl Mead looked at the two riders and had another fit of coughing, backing toward his wagon. He suddenly looked very ill.

Buck Hayden stood straight and tall. His face was hard and his eyes were cold. "Why don't you try killing just one of us, Leggett?" he said. "Why don't you try killing me?"

Skip Leggett went tense, glaring murder at him. "You don't think I can, Hayden?"

"That's right, I don't think you can." Then he added a deliberate taunt, "Not while I'm facing you."

Leggett blinked. "What's that supposed to mean?"

"It means I'm wondering how Frank Martin really died," Hayden said savagely. "He could have killed two or three of you in a fair fight."

Leggett snorted. "He never even killed one of us! And he was already holdin' this here scattergun with his thumb on the hammer!" He indicated the shotgun in his saddle scabbard.

"I don't believe you," Hayden said. "You either shot him when he wasn't looking or tricked him somehow."

A sly look crept into Skip Leggett's eyes. "You just ain't seen me draw yet, Hayden. And if you don't watch real close you won't see me at all. That's how fast I am. Cal, you remember how we got Martin?"

Cal Whitty did something to his horse and the animal began sidestepping nervously, moving farther away from Leggett's horse.

Skip Leggett was still watching Hayden. "You better not take your eyes off my hand, Hayden," he said, "or you'll never know what hit you."

Cal Whitty's horse suddenly reared.

A big pistol leaped into Hayden's hand and roared. Cal Whitty dropped the gun he had drawn and tried to hang onto the rearing horse, but fell heavily to the ground.

Hayden had already turned his gun on Skip Leggett. The curly-headed rider was caught off guard. His eyes, narrowed to glittering slits one moment, widened in alarm the next. His hand clawed at his gun, but it was only half out of the holster when Hayden's bullet lifted him from the saddle.

"My God!" Carl Mead gasped, holding his chest and staring in disbelief at the two dead men lying sprawled in the street.

"There something wrong with your heart too?" Hayden snarled. "If there is, you sure came to the wrong place. This country's bad on weak hearts, or didn't anybody tell you?"

Mead looked at him in wonder but said nothing.

Hayden punched the empty shells from his gun and thumbed in two fresh cartridges as he went forward for a closer look at the two dead men. He bent down over Cal Whitty and removed Frank Martin's cartridge belt and converted Starr, then got the shotgun and scabbard from Leggett's saddle and took it to his own, hanging the gun belt over the horn.

Boyle stood on his porch, shaking his head. Hayden crossed the street to the store and saw the scared look in the storekeeper's eyes.

"I'll need a couple boxes of .44s and some shotgun shells," the tall man said.

"You've played hell now," Boyle said. "Do you realize what this means?"

"Them boys needed killing," Hayden replied. "I couldn't see my way clear to leave the job for somebody else." He looked at the store-keeper through cold eyes. "Especially since there don't seem to be anybody else around here with the stomach for that sort of thing."

Boyle's eyes were wild. His mouth trembled and his voice shook when he said, "You're just making it hard on everyone! Hoffer's men will hunt you down like a mad dog! And when the shooting starts, no one will be safe!"

"Maybe you should have left with the other cowards," Hayden told him.

CHAPTER 3

Carl Mead drove his wagon out of town while Hayden was in the store. Hayden rode out a few minutes later.

He had bought some cigars at the store and he bit the end off one as he trotted past the new sign at the edge of town. Stacy stood beside the sign, red-faced and covered with white paint, glaring at him in silence. Hayden looked down from the saddle and grunted, "What happened to you?"

Stacy did not reply, but it appeared likely that, during the excitement a little earlier, he had fallen off his ladder and spilled the bucket of paint on himself. From the look on his face he evidently blamed Hayden for the accident.

Before long, Hayden thought bleakly, everybody in the whole country would be against him. Not just Hoffer and his men, but those who, like Boyle, wanted no trouble with the cattle baron and his tough crew. They wanted peace at any price, but it was a price Hayden could not afford to pay. A price he did not intend to pay. Not for Hoffer's brand of peace.

He soon overtook the wagon and plodding team, and reined the bay to a walk. Mead looked at him and coughed. That cough was beginning to annoy Hayden, mainly because he did not think it was really necessary. He hated to see a man who looked as healthy and fit as Mead pretending to be an invalid. He hated to think of what it was doing to Mead's wife, that tired looking woman he had seen yesterday at the old shack below the mesa. She looked older than Mead, although she was probably several years younger. Mead should be taking care of her, but evidently it was the other way around. Yet he was able to drive to town for supplies, stay there overnight and court the redheaded girl at the restaurant.

The cigar pulled Hayden's hard mouth down on one side, but even after he removed the cigar his mouth remained a little twisted with the scorn he could not help feeling for Mead. He looked at the man through cold eyes and asked, "You got a gun?"

Mead shook his head and coughed again. This time he did seem a little choked up, or perhaps merely embarrassed. Anyway, his face got red. "I was going to buy one, but Helen said I'd be better off without it."

"She's probably right," Hayden grunted. "Hoffer's men would just use it as an excuse to kill you and then claim it was self-defense."

He put the cigar back between his teeth and took a few puffs, his eyes on the mesa wall ahead. It was about twice as far away as it looked. Then his glance swept the rough country to the southwest where the isolated buttes loomed up hazy in the blowing dust. That was Hoffer's country down there. Of course, Hoffer seemed to think it was *all* his country, even though he did not actually own any of it.

"On the other hand," Hayden added, "going unarmed is no guarantee that they won't kill you. A few years back Hoffer tried the same thing in Texas that he's trying here. I was in West Texas at the time, quite a piece from there, but I heard about the trouble. He bought off a sheriff or two and at least one judge, and the law just stood by while he tried to drive everybody out of the country. Several men were killed and nothing was done about it. There was one old man who wouldn't fight or run either. Everybody knew he didn't pack a gun, so Hoffer didn't know what to do about him. Some of his men finally killed the old man." Hayden glanced at Mead on the wagon seat. "Shot him off his wagon. But somebody saw them do it and five of Hoffer's men were brought to trial. It wasn't much of a trial, though. They pleaded self-defense and got away with it. They claimed the old man reached inside his coat and they thought he was reaching for a gun. Here there's no law close enough for Hoffer to worry about, but I figure he's already bought off that fat sheriff over at the county seat, just to be on the safe side."

"Why did Hoffer leave Texas?" Mead asked.

"Killing that old man stirred people up against him. And some of the people he thought he'd run out of the country were just hiding in the brush, or rounding up their friends and relatives to help them get their land and cattle back. They made things so hot for Hoffer and his men that he decided to leave Texas. Here it looks like he's taken over the whole country without a fight. But what he don't know yet is that he didn't leave all the Texans in Texas. There's one here that he's going to be hearing from shortly."

Mead glanced curiously at him. "You from Texas?"

Hayden nodded. "I wasn't born there, but I think of myself as a Texan."

"Where were you born?"

"Missouri. But when I was ten my folks and Frank Martin's moved to Texas. Frank's ma drowned crossing a swollen river and my pa drowned trying to save her. When he saw her go down he was the closest one to her and I guess he forgot he couldn't swim. My ma ended up marrying Frank's pa, but a few years later they were both killed by Comanches and Frank and I were left on our own. Frank was a year older than me and always the steady one. I was restless and bad to fight when somebody made me mad, but he was always close by if I needed him and we usually came out on top, whether it was fists or guns. Frank was might handy with that old Starr pistol. He could shoot rings around most of the famous gunfighters you've probably heard of. But he kept it to himself, and most of the people who knew about it found out the hard way and they weren't alive to tell anyone."

"Could he shoot better than you?" Mead asked.

Hayden grinned. "I won't say about that. It might sound like I'm bragging."

"I don't see how he could have been much better," Mead said, his face a little pale. "I didn't even see you get that gun out back there in town. I didn't know who was shooting till it was all over and those two men were lying in the street."

After a moment he looked thoughtfully at Hayden. "Could you teach me to shoot like that?"

Hayden shook his head. "Not like that. You would of had to start a lot younger. You must be pushing thirty. Most gunfighters are either dead or thinking about hanging up their guns by the time they're your age."

"I notice you're still wearing yours," Mead pointed out. "And I'd say you're at least as old as I am, if not older."

"I may not be no older, but I've been around more. But I don't seem to be slowing down much yet. I'm just a little slower about getting started. Ten years ago I would of started shooting as soon as I saw them two with Frank's guns. I wouldn't have stood there and talked for five or ten minutes. It looks like I'm getting gabby in my old age."

Mead looked at the shell belt and holstered revolver hanging from Hayden's saddle horn. "Any chance you'd sell that pistol?"

Hayden drew the gun from the holster and checked the loads. It was an old gun, made before the Civil War, but in excellent condition and converted to use .44 centerfire shells. "I thought about loaning it to you," he said. "That's about what a greenhorn like you needs. You don't have to cock the hammer. Just point it at the target and squeeze the trigger. But there's something in what your wife said. A man who don't know how to use a gun is better off without one. You'd just get yourself killed. Your best bet is to pack up and get out of the country before Hoffer's men come back. I imagine they're about done talking."

Mead's jaw got stubborn. "That old shack doesn't belong to Hoffer. I've got just as much right to be there as him or any of his men. At first I was only planning to stay there for a week or two till we had a chance to rest up and the horses got in better shape, and then go on to California. But when his men came there and told us we'd have to leave, that's when I decided to stay. I don't take orders from men like them."

Hayden grinned. "Maybe I had you figured wrong."

"Maybe you did," Mead retorted.

Hayden lifted the gun belt from the horn and handed it to Mead, then slid the shotgun from the scabbard and passed it to him also. "Here's some shells for it. If you see any of Hoffer's men just put that scattergun across your lap. People get might uneasy around a shotgun. On the other hand, it didn't do Frank much good, if what Skip Leggett said was true, and he knew which end you fired it from. So if you get yourself killed, don't say I didn't warn you."

"If I get myself killed, I don't guess I'll be saying anything much," Mead said. "But what about you? I was sort of hoping you'd ride along with me the rest of the way."

Hayden's grin got brighter but colder. "I've got to pay a call to Mr. King Hoffer. There's a little matter of some missing money and horses that I want to ask him about."

King Hoffer sat behind a battered, boot-scarred desk in the room that he, like the former owner of the ranch, used for his private office. The unpainted frame house was not much compared to the plantation style mansion in Texas, but his experience there made him reluctant to build another fine house that he might have to abandon.

But he thought it unlikely that he would have to leave this place. He had picked his spot well this time, choosing the remote Nevada desert where there were only a handful of scattered ranches and most of them small. He had encountered no real resistance here except for Frank Martin and that fool of a greenhorn Mead. Martin was already dead and Mead soon would be if he did not wise up and get out while he had the chance. Hoffer had already given him his last warning. It seemed that the man called Hayden had come back, but he was a drifter and would soon be gone again. Hoffer foresaw no problem there.

He would soon have everything under control, it seemed, except for his daughter, or stepdaughter. She was as hard to manage as her mother had been, and even more beautiful.

He heard her humming quietly as she moved around in the next room and he raised his head to listen. He had a short thick neck and broad powerful shoulders. He was of medium height and rather stout. But except for a good deal more weight than he needed, he appeared well preserved for a man in his fifties. There was no gray in his short black hair, no lines in his dark face. Problems never worried Hoffer for very long. He just started looking for solutions and he soon found them, as a rule.

So far Rose was the only problem that had defied all his solutions. He still did not know what to do about her. A man or a horse he could have broken, and several times he had made up his mind to break her, but always he had failed. Just like her mother, he thought. Too wild to tame.

Hoffer had lost his first wife and child to cholera and had been in his thirties when he married Rose's mother. Perhaps he should have known he could not make her happy, and yet he had tried, in his way. Evidently he had failed.

His mind went back across time to a dark stormy night and a wild ride through the wind and rain, the slender dark-haired woman ahead frantically quirting her horse to get away. Going to meet the Mexican vaquero with whom she meant to elope, abandoning her husband and young daughter. That same reckless smiling vaquero who was really the child's father. It was not until years later, when he saw what a beautiful girl Rose was blossoming into, that Hoffer had started the story that his wife had been Mexican and that she had been married before to a white man who was the girl's father. In fact it had been the other way around. Rose's mother, though dark enough to be part Mexican or Indian, had been white; it was her father who had been Mexican, a fact Hoffer could not bear to think about.

Hoffer had moved after his wife's death and he had got rid of all the hands who knew the truth. One who had tried to blackmail him had died on the spot. None of the hands he had now knew how his wife and that Mexican had died on that stormy night almost twenty years ago. They only knew that he hated Mexicans and had long since got rid of all those he had working for him. He had made it clear that he wanted no Mexicans on his range.

And there too Rose had defied him.

Hoffer sat frowning at his desk for a moment, and then called quietly, "Rose, come in here a minute."

She opened the door and stood there frowning back at him, the color rising in her smooth tan cheeks. At times they behaved as if they hated each other. Yet Hoffer was sure that, in his heart, he loved her and he liked to think she felt the same toward him, though she hated to show it.

"Did you get rid of that greaser?" he asked.

The anger flashed in her large brown eyes. She tossed her dark head and her nostrils flared. "And what if I didn't?" she asked.

Hoffer's voice rose a little, his temper threatening to break out of control. "If you don't, then by God I will. I've already told you I don't want no greasers hanging around here."

"And what about me?" she demanded. "Am I not half greaser?"

He waved his hand impatiently. "That's different. You're my daughter. Do you think I don't know why he's here? I thought when we left Texas all those long-lost cousins of yours would quit turning up, but now it looks like they've even started coming all the way here to see you. It's going to stop now, before it gets started again, do you hear?"

"What if I said I'm in love with him?" she asked.

A wild look came into Hoffer's eyes. His voice was suddenly soft and deadly. "You better not be. I won't have you running off with no greaser, the way your mother did."

Her full breasts rose and fell with anger. "I don't think you want me to have anything to do with any man. You've already warned the hands to stay away from me, and I never get a chance to meet anyone else. You know what I think? I think you're trying to save me for yourself."

"Don't say that. You're my daughter. My stepdaughter, anyway."

"Then start behaving like a father instead of a jealous husband!" she yelled. "I don't like the way you look at me. It makes my skin crawl."

Hoffer half rose out of his chair, then settled back, breathing through his teeth. His voice shook with anger when he spoke. "You've seen something in me that's not there. I only want what's best for you. If a decent man came along, who would make you the right kind of husband—"

"You wouldn't let him get near me and you know it!" she retorted. "You'd run him off, the way you run off all those 'greasers,' as you call them."

He glared at her in silence for a time and them said softly, "I'll tell you one thing. You're not going to marry any greaser. And you're going to quit having anything to do with them. If you don't ask that one to leave, I'll ask him myself—and I won't be too polite about it. I don't want you sneaking out after dark to see him again, either."

"How will you stop me?" she asked, her lips twisted with scorn. "Lock me in the room?"

"If I have to."

She looked at him with hatred in her eyes and then flounced out of the room, slamming the door behind her.

"Rose!" he said sharply.

"Go to hell!" Then she added tauntingly, "*Father!*"

Hoffer started to get up and go after her, but just then he heard a knock at the front door. A minute later Rose was back, her beautiful face still twisted with scorn and a little pale except for spots of color in her cheeks.

"There's someone here to see you, *Father.*"

"Who?"

"Says his name's Hayden."

Chapter 4

When Rose was gone Hoffer settled back in his chair behind the desk and reached for a cigar, his face blank with surprise. He had not expected Hayden to come here. He had expected the man to leave the country as soon as he found out what had happened to Frank Martin and realized the same thing could happen to him. What could his coming here mean?

Hoffer listened. At first he heard only the wind rattling the leafless branches of the cottonwood outside his window, and it occurred to him that he had not heard a horse come up. Then he heard the quiet tread of boots approaching and a moment later the big man appeared at the door, his lips twisted in a wry, humorless grin, a hard bright gleam in his pale eyes as he looked at Hoffer.

Hoffer bit off the end of his cigar and waited, watching him carefully.

Hayden pushed his black hat back a little with his left hand and said, "You'll find a couple of your hands dead in town, Hoffer. They tangled with the wrong man."

"Who?" Hoffer asked sharply.

"Skip Leggett and Cal Whitty was the names they were using."

"I mean who did they tangle with?"

Hayden looked at him deliberately and said, "Me."

Hoffer glanced at the big man's guns, noticing that both of the holsters were tied down. As a rule, only gunfighters and greenhorns did that—and Hayden did not strike him as a greenhorn. "I see." He thoughtfully lit his cigar, keeping both hands where Hayden could see them. Then he shook the match out and said, "I've got a feeling you didn't ride out here just to tell me that."

Hayden's grin widened. "You're right, Hoffer. I want to know which one of your men killed Frank Martin and I want back the horses and money they stole."

Hoffer shook his head. "I don't know anything about any horses or money. But it was my understanding that Skip Leggett killed Martin. They went up there to see him about selling his claim, if he really had one, and he got after them with a shotgun."

"I was passing by that shack below the mesa yesterday when they showed up," Hayden said. "If Skip Leggett talked to Frank Martin the way he talked to that greenhorn's wife, I don't blame him for getting after them with a shotgun. I would have done worse than that."

"It looks like you did do worse than that," Hoffer said. His eyes hardened. "And I'd advise you to let the matter drop."

Hayden shook his head. "Not till I get back the money and the horses they stole. Frank had two good saddle horses and some mustangs he was gentling to sell. I helped him catch them and take the edge off them before I left."

"You won't find them here."

"What about that black stallion I just saw in your corral?" Hayden asked. "Frank Martin has been trying to catch that horse ever since he came here three years ago. I figured if anyone ever caught him it would be him."

Hoffer frowned. "You and Frank Martin just caught all his band and he came here trying to steal some of my mares to replace them. We managed to trap him in the corral, and my foreman broke his neck trying to ride him. Now the other hands are afraid to get near him. I wish I'd never seen the damn horse."

"I knew he'd be a hard one to break," Hayden admitted.

"As for the money," Hoffer added, "I don't know anything about it either."

"There was close to five hundred dollars in a tin can," Hayden told him. "When I got up there yesterday, both the money and the horses were gone. It was my money and I've got a paper to prove it. That was his idea, in case anything happened to him. Frank always wanted a real horse ranch, but we never seemed to get anything ahead mustanging. So every now and then I'd go off and work at something else for a while and send him the money or bring it back when I came."

"This is the first I've heard about you and him being partners," Hoffer said. "I thought you just helped him out when you were around, but you've been gone a big part of the time since I've been here. It's also the first I've heard about any money. If there were some horses in the corral, my men might have turned them out so they could get to grass and water. But if they had stolen five hundred dollars, I would have heard something about it by now. And all of them would have been drunk for a week." His hard eyes never left Hayden's face as he talked. "If you think you can come here with a story like that and I'll hand you five hundred dollars, then you've come to the wrong man. I don't bluff easy, and people who try to blackmail me get what they're asking for."

"I intend to get what I'm asking for," Hayden replied, "one way or another."

"I'm going to talk to my men about it," Hoffer said. His dark eyes glinted. "The ones you ain't already killed. But I don't believe there was any money, and if there was, somebody else stole it. I'm sure my men didn't."

"It sounds like you've got a lot higher opinion of them than I have."

"Don't get me wrong," Hoffer said. "They might do something like that, but they wouldn't have kept quiet about it. They would have told the other hands, and someone would have told me."

"If it wasn't them, who was it?"

Hoffer shrugged with complete indifference. Hayden had a feeling that he was telling the truth. "I have no idea. It could have been some stranger passing by. Or maybe that greenhorn Mead went up there and found it. He's closer than anyone else."

"He ain't the type," Hayden grunted. "He's too lazy besides."

"I don't know about that," Hoffer said. "People who hate work will do almost anything to get out of it. And him or somebody buried Martin. I sent my men back up there the next day to bury him, but the grave was already there. Whoever buried him prob'ly stole the money, if there was any to steal."

"I'm going to find out who stole it," Hayden answered. "And I'm going to find out who killed Frank Martin. If the killer ain't already dead, he soon will be."

Then Hayden turned on his heel to leave.

Rose Hoffer was in the next room, and it was obvious that she had been listening. That brought a smile to Hayden's face, and he saw the color rise in her cheeks when he removed his dusty black hat and bowed with mock courtesy. But the bold appreciation in his eyes was real.

"I don't see how a man like Hoffer could have a daughter like you," he said.

She looked at him with sudden interest and then said with a bitterness that surprised him, "I have often wondered about that myself. I don't see how he could even have a stepdaughter like me."

He paused to study her smooth beautiful face, admiring the way her long black hair fell over her graceful shoulders. "So you're only his stepdaughter?"

She nodded, watching him silently.

Hayden heard a rider coming up outside, and he could not think of anything else to say anyway. So he smiled again and went out with his hat in his left hand, keeping his right near his gun.

Stacy was just getting down from a heaving horse in front of the house.

"You again?" Hayden grunted in surprise. "You don't have to tell Hoffer about Leggett and Whitty. I already told him. You can go back and tell Boyle he sent you on a long ride for nothing."

Stacy only glared in silence, a look of near hatred in his eyes, and Hayden went on to his horse. Stacy stood and watched until the tall man had mounted up and ridden away. Then he knocked on the door and took off his paint-spattered hat when Rose Hoffer appeared. He soon found out that Hayden had told him the truth. Hoffer already knew about Skip Leggett and Cal Whitty.

"Go back and tell Boyle to bury them for me," Hoffer said. "My men are too busy."

"I reckon I know who'll do the buryin'," Stacy growled as he headed for the door.

"If you see Pete Grimes, tell him I want to see him," Hoffer called after him.

"Sure thing, Mr. Hoffer," Stacy said almost savagely. "I just hope he ain't too busy to come and see what you want."

When Hoffer sent for a man he came, no matter how busy he was, and a short time later Pete Grimes stood before the desk, nervously twisting his old hat in his hands.

"That mustanger was here," Hoffer said. "Buck Hayden. He said he killed Skip Leggett and Cal Whitty."

"That's what Stacy told me," Pete said. "I didn't believe it at first."

"I guess it's true or Boyle wouldn't have sent him out here to tell me. There's no reason why Hayden would lie about it either. I'm just wondering if he lied about something else." He studied Grimes with hard eyes. "He said you boys stole Martin's horses and some money that was in a tin can. Close to five hundred dollars."

Pete's eyes widened in surprise. "We turned the horses out of the corral and chased them off, and them boys went inside to see what they could find. But they never found no money, 'cause I stood at the door and watched."

Hoffer heard the back door slam as Rose went outside for something. He listened for a moment, and then said, "Maybe there wasn't any money. Maybe Hayden just made up that story about it because he figgers I owe him something." Then he asked, "You got any idea who buried Martin?"

Pete shook his head. "I don't know who it could of been."

"Think it was the greenhorn, Mead?"

"I guess it could of been. But it would be purty hard to get a wagon up on that mesa, and I don't think he ever rides a horse. I can't picture him walkin' up there. It's close to five miles."

"You see any tracks around there?"

"If you remember, it rained purty hard that night, and when we got back up there the next mornin' all the tracks was washed out. But it didn't look like there'd been anybody at all around there, except for Martin's body bein' gone and that grave. Skip said it was mighty considerate of that mustanger to bury hisself and save us the trouble. That was just his way of jokin'. You know how old Skip was."

Hoffer's eyes glinted. "Well, he's dead now. And something will have to be done about it. If we let Hayden get away with that, it might give somebody else the wrong idea." He hesitated. "Who's the best man here with a gun?"

"Tony Bick, I reckon."

"He as good as Skip Leggett was?"

"He's a lot better than Skip was," Pete said. "A lot of talk was about all Skip was. He was always starting something with his big mouth, but it was usually Tony Bick or some of the other hands who stepped in and finished it for him."

"I figgered something like that," Hoffer admitted. "But he sure could talk tough and he was good at throwing a scare into squatters and such. That's the only reason I didn't get rid of him a long time ago." Hoffer waved his hand impatiently, not wishing to waste time on idle talk. "Pete, you round up Tony Bick and some of the boys and go after Hayden. I don't guess I have to draw you any pictures."

Pete Grimes's sunburnt face turned pale and then got even redder than before. "I wish you'd send somebody else," he said. "I don't reckon I'm cut out for that sort of thing. I ain't slept much since Frank Martin was killed."

"Then get off my range," Hoffer said harshly, "and stay off. I won't have a man around me who ain't got the guts to do whatever has to be done."

Pete Grimes was a little frightened by the look on Hoffer's dark face. His voice was not quite steady as he said, "I got nearly a month's pay comin'."

"Never mind that," Hoffer barked. "Maybe you boys really did steal that money and divide it up between you. There's no telling how much this will cost me before it's over. Just be glad I'm letting you leave with your hide." He leaned forward over the desk. "Let me make one thing clear before you go. If you start running your mouth after you leave here, sooner or later I'll hear about it and I'll send someone to get you. Do you understand me?"

"I knew that all along," Pete said.

"Just so we understand each other." Hoffer waved his hand, dismissing him. "Find Tony Bick and tell him I want to see him before you go."

Pete Grimes nodded his head and left the room. He did not see Rose as he went out. It was just as well. He did not feel like saying goodbye, although he longed for one final glimpse of her.

He found Tony Bick drinking coffee in the cookshack and told him what Hoffer had said. It seemed to amuse Tony when he found out that Pete had been fired, nor was he upset by the news that Skip Leggett and Cal Whitty were dead. He was a little twisted in some way and always seemed delighted by the misfortunes of others, even those who thought of him as a friend.

A few minutes later Bick stood grinning before Hoffer's desk.

Hoffer frowned. "Pete tell you about Skip and Cal?"

"Yeah, he told me."

"I guess you know what it means," Hoffer said, still frowning.

Tony Bick's grin got even broader, showing his big white teeth. "We go after Hayden."

Hoffer nodded. "Take four or five men with you and start the first thing in the morning. And if you see that greaser sneaking around here anywhere, get rid of him too. Warn him the first time, and if that don't work, try something else."

"It'll be a pleasure," Tony Bick said. "I never did have no use for greasers. And mustangers is just as bad."

CHAPTER 5

From a rocky ridge Hayden watched his back trail, and after a time he saw the lone rider coming.

Pete Grimes reined up in surprise when Hayden stepped out with a gun in his hand.

"I didn't figure on just one man," Hayden said grimly, "and I didn't figure it would be you."

"I ain't lookin' for no trouble," Pete said quickly. "I told Hoffer I didn't want to go after you and he fired me. Never even paid me the wages he owed me. Said maybe we took some money from Martin. That's one reason I follered you. I wanted you to know what happened up there that day and to tell you it wasn't my idea, so you wouldn't come after me."

"What did happen?" Hayden asked, still holding the gun in his hand but not pointing it at Grimes.

Pete shrugged. "Skip Leggett did most of the talkin', but it was Tony Bick who killed him. He was off to one side a piece and while Martin was watchin' Skip, Tony pulled out his gun and shot him."

"I figured something like that. Skip Leggett and Cal Whitty tried to pull the same trick on me in town."

Pete Grimes looked back the way he had come and then folded his hands on the saddle horn, shivering in the cold wind.

"I went up there with them, but only because Hoffer sent me," he said. "I never took no part in what happened. After Tony shot him, they turned the horses out and then went inside to see what they could find. But they never found no money. All they took was his guns and shells."

"There was close to five hundred dollars in a coffee can," Hayden told him, "and somebody took it."

"I remember seein' a can like that lyin' on the floor with the other stuff," Pete said, "but I don't think there was no money in it. If them boys had found any, I would of seen them flashin' it around."

Hayden was silent for a moment, wondering if Frank had decided to hide the money in a safer place. If so, he must have been expecting trouble, and now that he was dead the money might never be found.

Then Hayden asked, "You have any idea who buried him?"

Pete shook his head. "Hoffer asked me that, but I don't know who it was. When we got back up there the only thing we found was that grave. Somebody must of buried him and then left before the rain stopped, or we would of seen the tracks."

"I don't think it would have been Mead up there in the rain," Hayden said. "So it was probably just some stranger who decided to clear out before somebody came along and started asking questions he couldn't answer."

An odd look came into Pete Grimes's eyes. "I just thought of somethin'. Rose Hoffer went for a ride that night with that greaser who's been sneakin' around and didn't get back till late. Hoffer was ready to send ever' man on the ranch out to look for her when she finally come in soakin' wet. But I don't guess they would of been way off up there at that old shack on a night like that."

Hayden rode into the yard at the Mead shack a little after dark and Mead appeared at the door with the shotgun in his hands.

"Easy," Hayden grunted. "It's me."

He got down, loosened the cinch and let the horse drink at the trough, then went toward the door. "I shouldn't have given you that scattergun," he said. "If Hoffer's men come around and see you standing in the door with it, they'll take it as a signal to start shooting. With you standing there in the light, they wouldn't have much trouble hitting you."

"I thought I heard something just before you rode up," Mead said. "I was just going to take a look around. Go on in. I'll be back in a minute."

"Be careful with that thing," Hayden grunted.

He glanced over his shoulder as he went in through the door, and then he saw Helen Mead watching him with a look of worry in her tired eyes.

"You're right," she said. "You shouldn't have given him those guns. If he tries to fight Hoffer's men they will kill him, or he'll catch his death going out to look around every time he thinks he hears something. He's not well enough to be going out in that cold wind."

Hayden frowned. "I don't think there's anything wrong with your husband, except a bad case of laziness. He only coughs when he looks at someone. If his lungs bother him, it's probably because they're just raw from coughing when he don't really need to."

She looked at him in surprise and then glanced toward the open door. She was silent a moment and seemed to be listening for some sound outside. Then she said in a low thoughtful tone, "I've had the feeling at times that he was pretending to be sick to get out of doing any work or trying to make a living."

"I've been wondering about that," Hayden said. "What does he do for a living?"

Helen Mead blushed. In the lamplight a faint down showed on her cheeks. "He's never done much of anything," she admitted reluctantly. "He used to come to a restaurant where I worked in Chicago, and I went on working there after we were married."

"He seems partial to waitresses," Hayden remarked, thinking of the red-haired girl at the restaurant in town.

Mead coughed in the yard and a moment later he came in and stood the shotgun in the corner by the door. He looked at Hayden with hard eyes and the latter guessed he had overheard the remark about waitresses. Hayden stared back at him and Mead was the first to look away. He glanced at the table where the lamp guttered in the drafty room, and then he smiled and said, "You can eat with us. Supper will soon be ready."

Hayden raised a hand to his face and felt the day-old stubble. "That side meat sure smells good," he said.

He glanced at the few pieces of travel-scarred furniture in the large room. A small cookstove, a bed, a washstand with a bucket and a basin, an old bureau in the corner. That was about all, and he suspected that they had not had much more in Chicago. A waitress with a husband to support—they could not have had very much.

"You plan to stay?" Hayden asked while they ate.

Mead looked up and grinned sheepishly. "I like it here," he said.

Hayden wondered if the waitress at the restaurant in town had anything to do with his decision. "You better take my advice and clear out," he said. "You can't fight Hoffer's men. I only came by to see if you were still here. I saw Pete Grimes earlier and he said Hoffer fired him because he didn't want to come after me. He was on his way out of the country and you should be too."

Helen Mead's eyes were worried. She had already quit eating, but remained at the table watching the two men while they ate. "I've been trying to get him to leave," she said. "But he's been talking about staying here and helping you fight Hoffer's men."

Hayden looked sharply at Mead, and the latter asked, "You think they'll come after you?"

Hayden nodded. "Hoffer tried to send Pete Grimes and some men after me, and Pete said he didn't figure anything had changed except Tony Bick will be leading them instead of him. That makes it a lot worse. Pete Grimes might not have tried very hard to find me. Tony Bick won't stop till he does. But I'll go back and make sure they don't trail me here. While I'm keeping them busy you better pack up and clear out. This ain't no place for greenhorns."

Tony Bick and four others rode out at dawn. The others were all older men than Bick, who was twenty-five. They did not like taking orders from him, but they kept their thoughts to themselves, for they were all a little afraid of the tall rider with the stringy blond hair and bright blue eyes. He was always looking for an excuse to use his white-handled gun. If you crossed him, from that moment on he would be trying to goad you into a fight. Or he might just kill you on the spot, with no warning whatever. That was the kind of man Tony Bick was.

It would be just their luck for Hoffer to make him foreman over them, especially if he was successful at hunting Hayden down and killing him. Hoffer had not yet replaced Sam Epson, who had broken his neck falling off that wild stallion, nor was it known whom he had in mind. Pete Grimes had been top hand, but now he was gone, and it seemed unlikely that he would have been tough enough to handle the kind of men who rode for Hoffer.

Tony Bick *was* tough, and he never passed up a chance to prove it.

They had not gone a mile when Bick drew rein and said, "Look what we got here."

The others blinked the sleep from their eyes and saw the Mexican just climbing his horse out of an arroyo. He saw them and halted, then came on and reined in before them, an embarrassed smile on his handsome dark face. He nodded his big sombrero at them and said, "*Buenos dias, señores.* Good morning."

Tony Bick grinned. "It sure is, greaser. But not for you. Hoffer don't want you sneaking around his daughter. You *sabe?*"

The Mexican laughed, his embarrassment more apparent. He seemed unable to think of anything to say.

"Better get started," Tony Bick said. "It's a long ride back to Mexico."

The Mexican's smile faded and he went tense, anger clouding his face. The crimson sun rimmed the mesa to the east, throwing his dark shadow across their path. For a long moment he sat motionless and silent in his saddle, staring at them from under the wide brim of his hat. Then he relaxed and shrugged his shoulders. "All right," he said, "I go."

He turned his horse and rode back the way he had come, dropping from sight again in the deep arroyo.

"You boys ride on a piece and wait for me," Tony Bick said, watching the arroyo. "I'll be along in a few minutes." He grinned. "This won't take long."

The others rode on along the trail, watching Bick curiously as he kneed his horse toward the arroyo. He got down, left the horse and walked the last fifty yards.

The Mexican had dismounted and was holding a hand over his horse's nose as he listened to the fading racket of the Crown riders. When he became aware of Tony Bick standing on the rim of the arroyo, he looked up, his dark eyes widening in alarm.

Tony Bick bared his teeth in a deadly, wolfish grin. "It looks like you don't *sabe* English so good, greaser," he said. "Maybe you'll *sabe* this."

Before the Mexican could move, Tony Bick drew his gun and shot him. The Mexican spun around and fell facedown in the deep sand of the arroyo.

Then Bick killed the horse. The horse required two bullets, the man only one.

CHAPTER 6

Hoffer rarely ate with the crew. He preferred to take his meals in the main house with Rose, and they were meals that she had cooked herself. Hoffer believed that if he kept her busy in the house she would have less time to go riding. He had no peace of mind when she was out of his sight. He had warned the men to stay away from her, but that Mexican had so far managed to avoid him so he could not tell him. Well, that problem would soon be taken care of.

At breakfast that morning she sat opposite him as usual, the sunrise flushing her cheeks through the window. She suddenly raised her dark head and said, "Listen. I thought I heard a shot."

"Probably one of them fools checking his gun and let it go off," Hoffer grunted. "Or maybe took a shot at a jackrabbit. Ain't a one of them got a lick of sense. I wish to God Sam Epson hadn't got his neck broke fooling with that crazy horse. He was the only man I've had in years that I could rely on."

She watched him with accusing eyes, not even listening. "You sent them after Hayden, didn't you?"

The rancher's own eyes hardened. "What if I did? He killed two of my men."

"Because they tried to kill him," she retorted, rising from the table and taking her plate to the sink. "And I hope he kills the ones you sent after him. He may do it too. He looked big and tough enough. Your men are no match for him. You can't get fighting men for what you pay them. They think they're tough, but wait till they tangle with Hayden. You should have kept more men this winter. You may need them."

"You let me worry about Hayden," Hoffer said. He noticed that she had on her riding clothes. "You just mind your own business. And stay away from that greaser. Next you'll be trying to run off with him."

"If I did it would only be to get away from here," she said. "And away from you."

The others stopped and waited when they heard the shots. A short time later Tony Bick rode up, looking quite pleased with himself.

"What happened?" asked Hoke Kelsey, a big tough looking man with a dirty beard and dark brows knitted in a permanent scowl.

Tony Bick smiled. "Nothing," he said. "Nothing at all."

Kelsey indicated the ground. "The wind has about covered these tracks with dust, but it looks like Pete Grimes was follerin' Hayden. You figger old Pete decided to take him on by hisself?"

"Not likely. He didn't even want to go along with us. That's why the old man fired him."

Hoke's scowl deepened. "Then what you figger it means?"

Tony Bick shrugged, then smiled. "Maybe Pete decided to tell him who killed Frank Martin."

"Who did kill him?" Hoke asked. "The way Skip Leggett was braggin', I just figgered it was him."

Bick shook his head. "No, it looked like Skip was going to talk all day and I kept noticing some clouds getting blacker and blacker. So I decided if I didn't do something quick we'd still be up there when it started raining."

Kelsey looked at him through narrow eyes. "So it was you who killed him?"

Bick nodded. "Now let's go get Hayden."

"It may not be as easy to get him."

"Hayden ain't no better than Martin was," Tony Bick said. "He may not even be as good."

They went on in silence. A gust of wind rattled the stunted desert shrubs, then the wind began blowing steadily, whipping dust into their slitted eyes. The mesa loomed before them, looking much closer than it was.

They quit bothering to look for tracks, for they believed they knew where Hayden had gone.

The sun shone directly into their eyes, streaming through the dusty haze. Whitey Cruger got something in his left eye and began blinking it angrily, the other pale eye glaring ahead with an insane glitter. Whitey Cruger almost never said anything. The other hands believed he was going mad or already there and avoided him as much as possible. But he was good with a gun, afraid of nothing, and that was why Tony Bick had picked him.

Tony had picked the others for the same reason, but he was beginning to doubt his judgment. For the closer they got to the mesa the clearer it got that they were scared. Their weather-beaten faces were gaunt and drawn, and they looked ahead with haunted eyes, as if they expected to find Frank Martin's ghost up there waiting for them.

Hoke Kelsey spoke again after a long silence. "Seems like one time I heard about a fight Hayden and Frank Martin was in. They shot four or five men to doll rags and didn't even get a scratch theirselves."

"You scared, Hoke?"

Hoke's eyes darkened with anger. "I ain't never seen a man yet I was scared of," he said. "But I ain't no fool neither. And I make a bigger target than the rest of you."

Tony Bick laughed. "You're scared all right."

In the middle of the desert there was a general store, its walls as bleak and gray as the mountains in the distance.

Inside, a tall gaunt-looking man in a battered old hat and a ragged coat stood looking at some revolvers in a glass display case. He had a short reddish beard and very cold blue eyes. For a long time he stood there staring at the guns in silence as though he hated the sight of them. At last he spoke reluctantly, like a man who did not care to talk.

"These the only guns you got?"

The man behind the counter nodded. "But I thought it was a pretty nice collection. I can let you have any of them second-hand guns real cheap. Most of them belonged to men who were down on their luck and traded them for supplies. But they're all good guns."

The tall man stood gazing at the guns in silence.

"See one you like?" the storekeeper asked hopefully.

The tall man pointed his finger. "Could I see that one?"

"Sure can, stranger. But that one will cost you a little more. It's nearly a new gun. Can't be very old, 'cause them double-action Smith & Wesson .44s ain't been out long."

The sun said midmorning when the Crown riders neared the mesa and saw Hayden sitting his red horse up on the rim in plain sight. They reined in at the foot of the steep rocky slope and sat their saddles looking up at him.

Hoke Kelsey muttered something under his breath. Tony Bick flashed his white teeth in a wicked grin. The others were silent and their eyes were uneasy.

Hayden's voice hit them like a whiplash. "You boys looking for someone?"

Tony Bick put his hands up beside his mouth and yelled back, "Yeah, you!"

"You've found me!"

Tony Bick grinned. "Why don't you come on down here a little closer, so we can get this over with! I want to get back in time for chuck!"

"I ain't one to keep a man from his chuck!" Hayden replied.

He drew the Winchester from his scabbard, let out a Rebel yell and sent his horse straight down the steep mesa slope toward them, raising a furious cloud of dust.

The Crown riders watched with big eyes, too startled to react at once. They had forgotten that he was a mustanger, which meant that he had followed wild horses wherever they went at a dead run—and wild horses thought nothing of galloping down what appeared to be sheer cliffs.

"Kill him!" Tony Bick cried, drawing his pistol.

Following his example, the others automatically reached for their own pistols.

"You can't hit nothing with them!" Bick snarled. "Use your rifles!"

Hoke Kelsey and the others reached for their rifles, and Hayden began firing. Bent low over the horse's neck, with the reins between his teeth, he rapidly worked the lever of his Winchester, spraying the air around them with lead. A bullet burned one man's ear. He yelled and jerked his horse around and headed for a safer place. The others followed in a wild panic, trying to get away from the screaming bullets. Tony Bick found himself alone, waiting for Hayden to get within range of his pistol. Then he turned his horse and followed the others, cussing them and their mothers and everyone else he could think of.

Had they been mustangs Hayden would have gone after them, but he figured men like them were not worth chasing. He got his horse stopped near the foot of the mesa and called after them with a grin, "Hope you boys enjoy your chuck!"

After debating a moment, he put the bay back up the steep mesa slope at an unhurried walk. From the rim he saw the dust raised by the Crown riders as they headed for home.

Hayden decided to cross the mesa to the Mead shack and see if Carl Mead had taken his advice and cleared out.

Hoffer leaned forward over the desk, staring in amazement at Tony Bick's flushed face. "Let me get this straight. You let Hayden chase all five of you back here with your tails between your legs?"

Bick's grin was gone and his teeth were bared in a bitter grimace. His red face twitched with almost unbearable rage at his failure, which he blamed on the cowardice of the men who had gone with him. "Them bastards turned tail and ran when they saw him coming. They were nearly back to the ranch before I caught up with them."

Hoffer snorted. "It sounds like you were riding pretty fast yourself!"

"Hayden had a rifle and all I had was a handgun. He would of killed me before he got close enough for me to get him."

"Then maybe you better start packing a rifle!" Hoffer roared.

"I've never used one," Bick said. "I never needed one before. And all them others had Winchesters, so I didn't figger I'd need one today."

"I pay you men top wages because I thought you were tough," Hoffer said savagely. "I thought you could handle any trouble that came up. But all five of you ran from just one man!"

"Well, you won't have to worry about that greaser anymore," Bick said. "I took care of him."

"Shut up, you fool!" Hoffer hissed.

Rose Hoffer suddenly appeared at the door behind Bick. Her face was pale. She had heard. "What does he mean, he took care of that greaser?" she asked.

"So you were listening," Hoffer growled. "As usual!"

"Yes, I was listening! You try to keep me cooped up in this house, so I listen every chance I get!" she said, her voice rising. "And I want to know what he meant!"

"I told him to run that greaser off," Hoffer said.

She was looking at Tony Bick, who had turned to stare at her in surprise. "I don't think that's what you told him," she said. "I think you told him to kill him! And I think that's what he did! I can see it in his eyes!"

Her own eyes, wide and dark and tragic, suddenly filled with tears. Her mouth twisted with bitterness and hatred. She started to say something else, but then only shook her head and fled from the room. She ran through the house and slammed the back door.

"You fool!" Hoffer yelled, glaring at Tony Bick.

"How the hell was I to know she was eavesdropping?" Bick asked.

"You've played hell now!" Hoffer said. "I told you to warn that greaser first, anyway!"

"I did warn the bastard. But he hid in a gully to wait till we were gone. I figger them two were planning to run away together the first chance they got."

"It wouldn't surprise me," Hoffer admitted. "I've caught her looking out the window a dozen times today, watching for him, I guess. She would have gone to meet him if I hadn't given her strict orders not to." His eyes filled with an old bitterness. "Just like her mother."

He cleared his throat and stared hard at Tony Bick. "Well, what's done is done. I don't blame you for killing the greaser, but I thought you had sense enough to keep your mouth shut about it here in this house."

Bick opened his mouth to speak. Hoffer waved a hand to silence him. "Never mind that now. Just finish the job I sent you to do. Take every man who can hold a gun and this time don't come back till you get Hayden. I don't care how many of you he kills, the rest of you stay and finish the job! Or by God I'll kill you myself!"

CHAPTER 7

Rose Hoffer ran to the bunkhouse and opened the door. Several men sat on their bunks, staring at her in surprise, for as a rule she went out of her way to avoid them and they had strict orders to stay away from her.

"Where is Francisco?" she demanded.

Hoke Kelsey scowled. "Who?"

"The greaser!" she cried bitterly, fighting back tears. "I know he's dead! What did you do with him?"

Hoke Kelsey was not very bright. "I never done nothin' with him. I guess he's still in that arroyo where he was hidin'."

She slammed the door and ran to the corral, caught her sorrel and began saddling him.

Hoffer appeared at the house door, filling it with his bulk. Tony Bick was just crossing the yard to the bunkhouse, and turned his eyes curiously toward the girl.

"Where do you think you're going?" Hoffer roared.

"You go to hell!" she cried over her shoulder, and began tightening the cinch.

Anger swelled Hoffer's chest and contorted his face. "I won't have you talking that way to me! I'm your father!"

"You're not my father!" she retorted. "And even if you were, I'd disown you!"

She swung astride the sorrel.

"Get down off that horse!" Hoffer bellowed. "You're not going anywhere!"

"Try to stop me!"

"Tony!" Hoffer bawled. "If she tries to leave, kill that horse!"

Tony Bick turned to look at him, wondering if he really meant it.
That sorrel was the best horse on the ranch, besides Hoffer's dark
chestnut. Rose cared more for her horse than she did for Hoffer.

The girl was already galloping past the silent gun hand.

"You heard me!" Hoffer shouted. "Shoot him!"

Tony Bick shrugged and drew his gun. He shot the horse through
the head, the second horse he had dispatched in one day. Rose's and
the Mexican's.

The sorrel grunted and turned a somersault. Rose sailed through
the air and rolled through the dust.

When the dust cleared the girl and the horse lay still on the
ground, about ten feet apart.

Hoffer made an odd sound in his throat. For a moment he seemed
stunned. Then he ran out to where the girl lay and stood looking
down at her.

"Rose?" he said. "Are you all right?"

The girl did not move or make a sound.

Tony Bick put away his gun and went toward them. Hoffer looked
around at him with wild eyes and said, "I should have locked her in
her room before this happened. I knew she'd try to run off with that
greaser. Just like her mother."

He bent down to lift the girl in his arms. But she suddenly rolled
away from him and got to her feet. Her clothes were dirty from the
fall, but she did not seem to be badly hurt. She had only been stunned
for a moment, the breath knocked out of her. She looked at the dead
horse and tears filled her eyes.

"You'll regret this," she told Hoffer.

He stepped toward her, holding out a big hand that trembled
slightly. "Rose, are you all right?"

She moved quickly away from him. "Don't touch me!" she said.
"Don't come near me! You won't have to lock me in my room. *I'll* lock
me in my room. And you keep out of it, you hear!"

She went to the house and slammed the door. She was limping
slightly.

The black stallion, excited by the shot and the smell of blood, was
circling the small corral where he was confined by himself, trying to

find a weak spot in the high pole fence. Hoffer glanced that way in silence, then indicated the dead sorrel.

"Tell a couple of men to drag him off," he said. "And bury that Mexican. But don't bring him around here." He looked toward the house with haunted eyes. "She's upset enough already."

Tony Bick gazed unhappily at the dead sorrel. Shooting the horse had been easy. Dragging him off would not be so easy, not even with horses and ropes, and it would take time.

"I thought you wanted us to go after Hayden," he said.

"I do," Hoffer growled. "But you can do this while you're waiting for the other men. Send someone to round them up. Take everyone but the cook this time. Cooks are hard to replace. If you can't get Hayden with ten men, I guess I'll have to go after him myself."

Tony Bick silently glanced at the gun belt cinched around Hoffer's thick waist. The rancher was getting so fat he could barely climb on a horse. About all he rode these days was that chair behind his desk. But he was as mean and tough as an old bull, as stubborn as a mule, and if Tony Bick and the others failed again, Hoffer might very well go after Hayden himself.

Hayden stopped at the Martin shack and filled a sack with canned food and other provisions. If he left it here, sooner or later Hoffer's men would steal it or destroy it. He tied the sack to his saddle horn, mounted up and glanced at Frank's grave with somber eyes.

In the sunlight the grave was nothing but a low mound of earth rapidly assuming the dun-gray color if the mesa. It was hard to believe Frank was even in the grave. No matter how far Hayden had gone in his restless wandering, he had never felt farther away from Frank than he did now.

It was not the same at night. Hayden had spent most of last night in the shack, but he had slept very little. Several times he had felt sure there was someone creeping around outside, although he had heard no one. Nor had he believed it was Hoffer's men. He had almost wondered if Frank Martin's ghost had returned to haunt the place. Yes, there for a while in the night, with the old house creaking in the wind, Hayden had almost believed in ghosts. It had not seemed a very friendly ghost either. Not that the ghost had done anything. It was just a feeling Hayden had—a feeling that something deadly was lurking nearby.

He studied the grave thoughtfully for a time, then rode on east

across the mesa, thinking about Frank Martin and all they had been
through together. In many ways they had been closer than most
brothers, and yet he realized that he had never known Frank very
well. The man he remembered had been a stranger. Frank had kept
his thoughts to himself. At times he had been very witty, but it was
a wry, twisted sort of wit and he had rarely spoken more than a few
words at a time. Around strangers he had said almost nothing, and
they had instinctively avoided him, perhaps sensing the quiet deadliness in the man. To his enemies Frank had been deadly, and Buck
Hayden was the only man he had ever regarded as a friend.

As he rode Hayden kept his eyes busy, watching for Hoffer's men
and the horses they had set free. So far Hayden had seen no sign
that the horses were still on the mesa, and that seemed odd, if Hoffer and Pete Grimes had told him the truth. The mesa had been the
mustangs' range even before they were caught, and he did not believe
Frank's roan and buckskin would have strayed far. Hayden should
have seen them or their tracks by now, and he had not. The whole
mesa seemed deserted, as if every living thing had fled from it. It
made Hayden uneasy, and his eyes darted about as if he expected to
see something that was not there.

At the east rim he looked down on the Mead shack and scowled
when he saw smoke curling lazily from the rock chimney. The wagon
stood in the yard where it had been last night. The two horses grazed
peacefully nearby. There was no sign that the Meads were getting
ready to leave.

Hayden picked his way down a trail that was more suitable for a
mountain goat than a horse. But the bay was almost as sure-footed as
a mountain goat and Hayden gave him his head down the trail that
wound among huge boulders and stunted brush to the desert below.
The gelding took his time, stopping once or twice to paw the ground
before going on at a cautious walk. They dislodged a few small rocks
that rolled down almost to the shack and brought Mead out with the
shotgun. He was also wearing Frank Martin's old Starr belted about
his waist.

"Save it for Hoffer's men," Hayden called when Mead, half blind-
ed by the noon sun, started to raise the shotgun.

He rode into the yard, watching Mead with hard eyes, and said
roughly, "I thought I told you to clear out."

Mead's face got red and his voice shook with anger. "I don't take
orders from you any more than from Hoffer's men."

"It's them I'm thinking about," Hayden replied. "If they don't start having more luck with me, they're going to come down here and take it out on you. I've always tried to look out for fools and greenhorns, but I'm not going to let them kill me just so they'll go easy on you."

"I don't expect you to," Mead said.

Helen Mead appeared at the shack door. She looked pale and worried and she did not smile at Hayden, but her eyes were gentle. "You can eat with us," she said. "I'll soon have a bite ready."

Hayden grinned and got down from the saddle. "That's the best offer I've had all day."

"Go on in," Mead said. "I'll take care of your horse."

"Mighty hospitable," Hayden said, glancing at the house. "I'm going to miss you folks."

"We ain't left yet," Mead said.

Hayden pulled his Winchester from the scabbard. "I'm a patient man," he said. "It's Hoffer who's run out of patience. He can't let two little men like you and me stand between him and his dream."

"What is his dream?" Mead asked.

"He wants to own this whole country. He wants to be king here, and he's afraid we might pull him off his throne."

"Ain't it about time somebody did?" Mead said.

Hayden squinted thoughtfully at him. "It's way past time," he said. "But you ain't the man for the job. Next to me, Frank Martin was about the toughest man I ever knew, and you know what happened to him."

"I know the story Hoffer's men told in town."

Hayden glanced up at the boulder-strewn slope of the mesa. "I don't guess it matters much how they got him. The point is they did."

"Maybe he's not dead at all," Mead suggested. "Helen said she dreamed he was still alive."

Hayden's look of surprise changed to a skeptical grin. "If dreams meant anything," he said, "me and Rose Hoffer would of headed for California or someplace a long time ago. As it is, I've barely spoken to her."

"That's a start," Mead said.

Hayden smiled bleakly. "Don't handle that bay like no work horse. He might not like it." He would have preferred to take care of the horse himself, for he doubted if Mead knew how. But he saw that Helen Mead was waiting at the door as if she hoped for a word alone with him, so he went that way with his rifle and followed her inside.

She glanced through the doorway and then turned her anxious eyes to him. "When you leave," she said in a low tone, "take Carl with you. I can't protect him from those men. Maybe you can."

Hayden studied her face carefully, noticing the faint wrinkles around her faded eyes, the tired lines near her mouth. She looked older than he had thought. "That's an odd thing to say," he said. "I always figured it was the man who should protect the woman."

She flushed. "He can't protect me," she said. "He can't protect anyone, not even himself. If he tries to he'll just get himself killed. You know that as well as I do. He doesn't know how to use those guns you gave him. If Hoffer's men come here and he tries to stand up to them, they will kill him."

"What about you?" Hayden asked.

"I don't think they will bother me, if he's not here," she said. "One of them made some remark as they were leaving here one day, and I heard the one they called Pete say they'd be crazy to bother me. He said if a man bothered a woman in this country, he'd have men after him that would usually run from a jackrabbit."

"Pete Grimes ain't with them no more," Hayden told her. "He was fired because he wasn't mean and tough enough to suit Hoffer. That should give you some idea what kind of men the others are, if you don't know already."

"I don't think they will bother me," she repeated. "When I worked at that restaurant I had some experience handling rough men and drunks. Usually I could just talk to them and they would behave themselves. But if Carl goes out with those guns, Hoffer's men won't pay any attention to me."

Hayden frowned. "I figure Hoffer will send his whole bunch after me the next time. I can't fight them and worry about a greenhorn at the same time."

"Then get those guns back before he gets himself killed," she said. "Or teach him how to use them well enough to protect himself."

Hayden shook his head. "He'd just get more guns in town. And I ain't got time to teach him how to use them. You might of read stories about greenhorns who came out west and became experienced frontiersmen and gunfighters overnight, but it don't happen that way. I can't teach him in one day what it's taken me a lifetime to learn. Your only hope of keeping him alive is to get him out of the country before Hoffer's men kill him."

"He won't go!" she exclaimed, her eyes desperate. "He won't even

discuss it. If I bring it up he just quits talking or goes outside somewhere. He's made up his mind to stay."

Hayden's frown deepened into a scowl. "He ain't even got a horse
fit to ride. I plan to keep on the move and not let Hoffer's men get
too close when they've got the edge. But if Mead tags along on one
of them old work horses, I'll either have to leave him behind or poke
along with him."

"Shouldn't some of Frank Martin's horses still be around there?"
she asked.

"Should be," Hayden agreed. "Both Hoffer and Pete Grimes said
they didn't steal them, just chased them off. But I'm beginning to
think they lied to me about that."

"If they stole your horses, then why don't you steal theirs?" Helen
Mead said.

Hayden looked at her as if seeing her for the first time. Her glance
did not waver. "You know what they do to horse thieves out here?" he
asked. "They hang them."

"They're already trying to kill you!" she exclaimed. "What differ-
ence does it make whether they use a gun or a rope?"

A wry, bleak smile touched Hayden's mouth. "You've got a point
there," he admitted.

CHAPTER 8

Hayden ate in scowling silence, wrestling with the problem in his head. Helen Mead watched him and her husband with anxious eyes, eating very little. Mead kept his eyes on his plate, his handsome dark face blank as usual. With a different background, he might have made an excellent gambler.

Then it occurred to Hayden that he knew very little about Mead's background, and he suspected that there was a good deal about him that his wife did not know. But that was often the way of it. There was probably a lot about her that Mead did not know.

After dinner Hayden stood at the door without his hat and bit off the end of a cigar, looking out at his rangy bay and Mead's heavier horses cropping the scant grass below the shack. His dark brown hair had a faint copper sheen in the sunlight. His nose was strong, the bridge a little high. His face was brown and rugged, but rather handsome if you overlooked what a rough life in the open had done to it.

He lit the cigar, then turned to get his hat and rifle and walked out into the yard. Mead followed but hung back a little. Helen watched them through the doorway with her silent worried eyes.

Hayden turned and frowned at Mead. "You got a saddle?"

Mead looked embarrassed as he shook his head. "When I went riding back home I rode bareback or rented a horse from the livery."

"You can ride, then?"

"Yes, I can ride." Mead was silent a moment, then he gave Hayden

55

a sheepish grin. "I always wanted to be a cowboy. I meant to come west a long time ago, but kept putting it off for one reason or another."

Hayden blew out cigar smoke and looked at him thoughtfully. "You sure you wanted to be a cowboy?" he asked. "Or a gunfighter?"

Mead coughed. "Both, I guess."

"You'll have to leave off that coughing if you're going with me," Hayden told him. "It will get us both killed. In this country a man has to keep mighty quiet at times or he won't last long."

"Where are we going?" Mead asked.

"We've got to get you a horse," Hayden replied. "Yours won't do. I guess Frank Martin's saddle is still in the shed. I didn't think to look. If it is, you can use it."

"When are we leaving?"

"Not yet for a while," Hayden said. "Let's see if you can shoot. Leave that scattergun here and bring that old Starr."

Mead leaned the shotgun against the wall and they walked out away from the shack. Hayden ran a narrow glance along the mesa rim and then said, "This should be far enough. Pick yourself a rock and see if you can hit it. Away from the house. Don't ever shoot toward a house unless you mean to kill someone. Even if it looks like it's been empty for years, some camper might be in it."

"Or some squatters like us," Mead said.

Hayden nodded without comment.

Mead looked about for a target, then drew the Starr from the holster, took aim and pulled the trigger. The pistol roared and almost jumped out of his hand. Mead looked startled, a bit shaken.

"Which rock were you shooting at?" Hayden asked.

Mead flushed. "Not the one I hit."

"That's what I figured," Hayden grunted. "Don't worry about speed at first. And don't jerk the trigger. Squeeze it. And don't let the gun wobble all over the place while you're doing it. Try cocking the hammer first. That will make the trigger easier to pull."

Mead thumbed the hammer back, raised the gun, squinted down the barrel and fired. The bullet kicked up dust and screamed off across the desert.

"I didn't do much better," Mead said unhappily, wiping sweat from his face.

He kept firing until the gun was empty, dotting a large ring around the rock he was shooting at. Then he reloaded and started over with a new rock for a target, but it was no easier to hit.

"I guess it's hopeless," Hayden concluded. "You took too much time and still didn't get anywhere near the target. But if there's a bunch of Hoffer's men, you might get one of the others even if you don't hit the one you're shooting at. I just hope I'm not anywhere in the same general direction when you cut loose with that thing."

They reached the shack on the mesa just as it was getting dark. After a careful look around, Hayden dismounted and stepped to the shed. There he halted, looking inside.

Mead, still on his horse, asked, "Is the saddle still there?"

"No, it ain't." Hayden entered the shed for a more careful look even though he knew it would be a waste of time. "I guess whoever took the horses took the saddle too."

"You think it was Hoffer's men?"

"I don't know," Hayden said in a puzzled tone, as he returned to his horse. "Hoffer might of lied about it, but somehow I don't think Pete Grimes would."

When he was back in the saddle he looked at the old shack with uneasy eyes, then swept the area with a searching glance. "This place gives me the creeps," he muttered, "since Frank's gone."

They slowly circled the shack and rode on west across the mesa. Mead watched the dark shack over his shoulder, his feet dangling below the horse's belly. "You think it's haunted?" he asked finally.

"I figure it's just a notion in my head," Hayden replied. "I imagine that's about all it usually amounts to when somebody gets the idea a house is haunted."

"I don't know," Mead said slowly. "Helen believes in ghosts and spirits and all that, and she gets feelings about things that usually turn out to be right."

Hayden grinned softly. "Did she get a feeling you'd be safer with me than at home with her?"

"Is that what she told you?" Mead asked.

"She said she couldn't protect you from Hoffer's men and maybe I could."

Mead was silent for a long moment. Then he cleared his throat and said, "Maybe she's decided she'd be better off without me. Maybe she thinks she'd be better off with you. I've seen how she looks at you."

Hayden shot him a quick look. "I hadn't noticed." He thought about it for a time, and then asked, "Does it bother you?"

Mead smiled. "It might, but I ain't seen you look at her the same way."

"Don't let it worry you," Hayden told him. "I saw the look in her eyes as we were leaving. She looked scared to death, and it was you she was worried about, not me."

Mead rode in silence, smiling a little in the gathering darkness. He seemed happy. He was doing what he had always wanted to do. He was riding off into the night with a gun on his hip, and he had a pretty wife who would be waiting for him when he got home.

Hayden was not so lucky. He had no wife, and he did not have Mead's comforting illusion that this was just a harmless game. He knew that either one or both of them might be dead before this night was over. Helen Mead might find herself a widow before sunrise.

What have I got myself into, Hayden wondered, bringing a green-horn along? It was her idea but if he gets himself killed, she'll blame me.

Then it occurred to Hayden that it had not been Helen Mead's idea at all. Carl had already made up his mind to stay here and help Hayden fight Hoffer's men, and realizing that she could not get him to change his mind, she had merely helped him to get his wish, even though her heart was frozen with fear and dread of what might happen to him.

"Ain't you curious about where we're going?" Hayden growled.

"I've been wondering about it," Mead admitted. "But I figured you'd tell me when you got ready."

"I aim to get me a stallion," Hayden told him. "When we get close to Hoffer's ranch, I aim to send you on back with my horse and that draft animal you're riding. I'll need both hands for the stallion."

The Crown riders were all in the bunkhouse, cleaning weapons and preparing for an early start the next day. An even ten men, including Tony Bick. They could not fail to get Hayden this time.

Bick was still bitter about what had happened that morning, but he hid his bitterness behind a deadly smile and tried to turn the fiasco into an amusing joke on the men who had been with him. He directed his ridicule at Hoke Kelsey, the one who seemed to resent it the most.

"Old Hoke nearly killed his horse trying to keep up with the others. It wasn't the horse's fault, Hoke, if you weighed about forty pounds more than any of the others."

One of the hands who had not been with them snickered, and Tony Bick bared his prominent white teeth in an appreciative smile.

Hoke Kelsey sat on his bunk, a murderous scowl on his bearded face. He had just cleaned and reloaded a huge revolver which he still held in his hand. For a moment he seemed to debate turning the gun on Tony Bick. The moment passed. He carefully put the gun away and said, "You sure wasn't far behind. Ever' time I looked back it seemed like you was gainin' on me."

"I was trying to get the rest of you stopped and turned around," Bick said. "Or borrow a rifle from one of you. But I never got close enough."

"I knowed you was yellin' somethin'," Kelsey admitted. "But I thought you meant for us to keep goin'."

Bick stared at him a moment in silence, then glanced at Whitey Cruger. "Whitey's the one who really surprised me. I didn't think he was afraid of anything."

"Couldn't see to shoot," Whitey grunted. "Got something in my eye."

The eye had been bothering Whitey all day. He could not keep from rubbing it, and the more he rubbed it the more it bothered him.

"Looks like you may lose that eye, Whitey," Tony Bick said with deliberate malice. "It's red as the inside of a bullet hole."

Whitey Cruger stood glaring at him in silence, his bloodshot eyes filled with hate.

Rose Hoffer sat on the edge of her bed in the dark, bent over rubbing her ankle. The ankle was sore and a little swollen, but did not seem to be badly hurt. She did not think anything was broken. She had been thrown from horses before, and had learned to fall so as to minimize the risk of serious injury.

She had eaten no supper, but was not hungry. Nor had she cooked anything for Hoffer. She had vowed not to leave her room while he was in the house, even if she starved. She had heard him in the kitchen earlier fixing himself a bite rather than go to the cookshack and eat with the crew, thereby admitting that he could not make her obey.

Now he was back in the room where he spent so much time, with a cigar between his strong teeth and his boots up on the desk, planning and scheming, dreaming his dream of an empire in this desolate wasteland so remote from all the things Rose wanted. She was determined to get away, but he was just as determined to keep her here. He could not bear the thought of her leaving and perhaps marrying some man. He wanted her for himself—she knew that even if he did not.

She thought of Francisco, perhaps still lying dead in that arroyo. Poor Francisco! Her eyes filled with tears. She had not loved him, but now she had no one. No one to take her away from this dreadful place and away from Hoffer. Francisco was the only man who had dared to get near her in a long time. And now he was dead.

There was no hope for her. Hoffer would keep her here forever, and she hated to think what might happen. Sooner or later he always got what he wanted. It was only a question of time. Now he sat in there like a fat spider, waiting for her to get trapped in his evil web.

She became aware of the sound of voices. She heard Hoffer exclaim softly, "What the devil! How did you get in? You must be insane coming back here. All my men are in the bunkhouse itching for a chance to kill you."

"Relax, Hoffer," a man said. "Keep your hands where I can see them. I didn't come here to kill you. Not this time. There'll be time enough for that later."

She recognized Hayden's quiet strong voice and she raised her head to listen, aware that her heart was beating faster. She had seen him a few times but had never really noticed him until yesterday, and yet now she could see him clearly in her mind. So tall and rugged and sure of himself. She could even see the twisted grin on his lean hard face. That grin had irritated her—and now she hoped it irritated Hoffer even more.

"Then what do you want?' Hoffer barked, his face no doubt turning purple with rage.

"Keep your voice down, Hoffer. It would break my heart if your men busted in here and you got shot. I ain't looking for no amusement. I'm here on business."

"What kind of business?"

"Horse business."

"I already told I don't know anything about your horses."

"It wasn't them horses I had in mind, Hoffer. I want that black stallion."

"That black stallion?" Hoffer echoed. "What in the world do you want with him? I figgered what you needed right now was a fast riding animal."

"That's just what I had in mind," Hayden replied. "That stallion can outrun anything you've got. I know, because he outran the best horses me and Frank Martin could find. All we ever saw was his dust."

"You're crazy!" Hoffer exclaimed. "No one can ride that horse!"

"Any horse can be ridden, Hoffer. All it takes is the right man."

Hoffer barked a short laugh. "I'll make a deal with you, Hayden. If you can ride that stallion away from here, he's yours."

"Put it in writing, Hoffer. All nice and legal."

"You don't trust me?"

"No," Hayden replied. "But it ain't you I'm worried about. If anything happens to you, I wouldn't want anyone to get the idea I stole the horse. Some people will jump at any excuse to hold a necktie party, especially if things have been dull for a spell."

"I don't think you need to worry about that," Hoffer growled. "You'll get your neck broke on that stallion, like Sam Epson did."

"In that case, maybe you wouldn't mind throwing in a saddle." An edge came into Hayden's voice. "Frank Martin's seems to have disappeared along with his horses."

"I don't know anything about that," Hoffer said. "But I'll throw in a saddle. It will be worth it. I want to see this!"

"You will see it," Hayden told him. "Because I want you out there where I can see you. If you try to warn your men before I get away from here, you'll be the first one who gets shot."

Rose found herself listening with breathless attention. She was even smiling a little. That Hayden was her kind of man. Afraid of nothing. And so big and strong. He gave the impression that he could do anything with ease.

She heard him say, "Leave your gun here, Hoffer, and walk out ahead of me. Nice and slow."

"You're holding the cards," Hoffer grumbled.

"Better yet," Hayden told him, "I'm holding the gun."

Rose sat tensely on the edge of the bed until they were outside and the house was silent. Then she got up and stepped quickly to the window. She drew the curtain aside and peered out. She saw them crossing the dark yard, Hayden tall and lean, Hoffer short and broad. If Hayden was holding a gun she did not see it in his hand.

They went toward the corrals and Hayden soon vanished in the shadows. But she could see Hoffer standing outside the small corral where the black stallion was. Then she heard the stallion scream his rage and pound about the corral. She could see him jumping and bucking furiously. Hoffer quickly let the bars down and the stallion exploded into the open with Hayden clinging to his back. They went racing across the yard and Hoffer suddenly bellowed like an enraged bull.

"It's Hayden! Get him! Kill him, you fools!"

The bunkhouse door burst open and men poured out in the lane of light from inside. A gun flashed and roared in Hayden's hand as he went by and the men scrambled back inside and slammed the door.

Then Hayden was gone, a black streak in the darkness. The thunder of the stallion's hoofs soon faded in the distance.

Hoffer threw his hat down and stamped on it in his rage.

Rose did not realize that she was clapping her hands and jumping up and down until her ankle began to hurt. Then she limped back to the bed and sat down. She sat there smiling in the dark.

At last, she thought. A man who is not afraid of him.

Chapter 9

The stallion headed straight for the mesa, his old stamping ground, without realizing that was where Hayden wanted to go.

Having failed to buck the man off, he now seemed to think he could escape by running, as he had always done in the past. But the man stayed on his back and the stallion snorted his rage. He tried to get away by leaping arroyos and tearing through the thickest and thorniest clumps of brush, but the man clung to him like an unwanted lover. The stallion felt violated and degraded.

Carl Mead plodded along off to one side. In the dark it was hard to tell which one of the horses he was riding and which one he was leading.

The stallion turned his head and pricked his ears in that direction. Here was another instance where his kind had been forced to serve the puny two-legged creatures who seemed to think they owned the whole world and everything in it. The stallion snorted his indignation and rage. He stopped in his tracks to glare at the gawky rider and to whistle a sharp command to that horse to pitch him off pronto and take out for the hills, make a break for freedom.

It did not occur to Hayden, at least not at the time, that the greenhorn Mead was in any way responsible for what happened. He had no time to think about it, but he just figured this was the stallion's latest attempt to unload him. And this time he very nearly succeeded, whether that was what he had in mind or not.

When the stallion stopped, Hayden kept going. But as he sailed forward he managed to hook one arm around the stallion's neck just behind the head, and he threw all his weight into the fall and gave a violent twist. The stallion went down with him and when the black came up screaming his fury Hayden was back in the saddle. The stallion believed Hayden had thrown him to the ground on purpose, as indeed he had, and he swung his head around and tried to bite the man's leg. Hayden brought up a boot and kicked the stallion on the jaw. The stallion screamed and again thundered across the desert toward the mesa, which he never should have left.

"Go on home!" Hayden yelled at Mead. "I'll be there when I get there!"

Mead gaped in silent wonder, and then muttered to himself when Hayden was gone, "He'll be there long before I will, the way he's going."

But it was a little after sunrise when Hayden rode up to the Mead shack. The stallion was unsteady on his feet, and when Hayden got off he staggered with weakness. Holding onto the reins, he swept off his hat and plunged his head in the watering trough. The stallion butted him out of the way and began drinking greedily. Hayden backhanded the animal sharply across the nose and pulled him away from the water.

"Damn horse will kill me yet," he grumbled as he sank to the ground. "Couldn't get him stopped till he wore both of us out circling the top of that mesa. Then he tried to lay down and roll on me as we were coming down off it."

Mead had come out with the shotgun. He glanced uneasily back the way Hayden had come. "What about Hoffer's men?" he asked. "Won't they be coming?"

Hayden nodded sadly. "They sure will. We better find ourselves a place to make a stand, if you're still set on getting yourself killed. Me and that stallion are both too wore out to outrun them. He used us both up last night. I can't leave him behind and he'll cause all kinds of trouble if I take him along. Don't ever ride a stallion if you can get anything else. Sometimes women ride mares, but only a fool rides a stallion."

"What else is there?" Mead asked.

"Geldings," Hayden told him. "That's the only thing to ride. Geldings."

Mead glanced at the stallion. "If you knew he'd be so much trouble, why did you get him?"

Hayden also looked at the stallion—through a haze of weariness and anger, mingled with grudging admiration. "I figured I might have to leave these parts sudden-like and I wanted to take him along. I want to get me a few good mares, use him for a stud, and start that horse ranch me and Frank Martin were always talking about. But I don't know where it will be. I've about wore out my welcome around here."

Helen Mead appeared at the shack door, looking drawn and tired as if she had not slept much. "I've got breakfast ready."

Hayden managed a weak grin. "Seems like I always get here just in time to eat, don't it?"

Her anxious eyes lit up in a smile.

Mead also smiled. "I think you time it that way on purpose."

"Could be," Hayden admitted. "Your wife's a good cook. Even better than Frank Martin was, and he sure knew how to cook. Wasn't much he couldn't do better than anybody else. I'm sure going to miss him. If he was here now, I'd figure the odds were about even."

"What chance do you think you and I have got?" Mead asked.

Hayden glanced up at him. "About half as good as me and Frank would have."

Tony Bick swung into the saddle and looked at the others. He counted eight men, besides himself. It appeared that someone had deserted.

"Where's Whitey Cruger?" he asked.

Hoke Kelsey scowled. "I think he went to town to see if he could get somethin' for his eye. He said it was drivin' him crazy."

"If it hadn't been the eye, it would have been something else," Bick said. "He was overdue."

Somebody snickered. But most of the men were silent and solemn, and two or three of them shivered in the cold, their eyes haunted with fear. The suspicion was creeping among them that their luck had gone bad, that the outfit was jinxed. It was as if the killing of Frank Martin had brought a curse down on them all.

"Well, we can't wait for him," Bick said. "I meant to leave before daylight."

Hoffer stood at the house door, chewing on a dead cigar and watching them with bitter bloodshot eyes. He was thinking about last night. Hayden had made them all look like fools. He had heard Rose laughing about it in her room. That made it unbearable.

"Don't come back till you get him," Hoffer barked. "You've got my orders to kill any man who runs this time."

"Don't worry," Bick said. "We'll get him." He smiled scornfully at the others as they trotted out of the yard. "Won't we, boys?"

"Boys, hell," Hoke Kelsey growled. "I'm a good ten years older'n you."

"I saw what a big tough man you were yesterday, Hoke," Tony Bick said. "I also noticed what a broad back you had when you turned and ran. It would be mighty easy to put a bullet in it if you took a notion to do that again." He grinned. "And you know me, Hoke. I always follow orders."

Hoffer watched them until they were out of the yard, and then he stepped back inside and closed the door, hugging himself against the morning chill. He walked to the door of Rose's room, raised his fist and knocked. "You might as well come down off your high horse," he said. "It won't do you no good to stay in there and starve."

"I already came down off my horse," she retorted. "Or have you already forgotten?"

"I'm sorry about the sorrel," he said. "But I'll get you another horse, one you'll like even better."

"There's no horse in the world that can take that one's place," she said bitterly. "I raised him from a colt. And what good would it do to get me another horse anyway? You never want me to go riding. You've got so you don't want to go anywhere yourself because you're afraid I might go for a ride while you're gone and meet someone, or that someone might come here to see me."

He had not realized it was so obvious, but he reflected that she was a very bright girl, in her way. "Well, I've had some experience along that line with your mother," he said. "And you too, when it comes to that. She ran off with a penniless greaser and it looked like you were getting ready to do the same."

"So you had him killed!"

"Tony Bick overstepped his orders. Or misunderstood them. I only meant to run that greaser off, not kill him."

"Ha! And what about the greaser who ran off with my mother? You killed him yourself, didn't you?"

For a long moment Hoffer stared at the door without seeing it. "Who told you that?" he asked finally.

"I heard it a long time ago," she said angrily. "Did you think you could keep something like that a secret?"

Hoffer's lip trembled when he spoke. "If you'd been there you would of understood. Her horse stepped in a gopher hole and threw her. She was dead before I got to her, and there was that greaser crying over my wife—my wife—like he had some right to! Yes, I killed him! And I'd do it again!"

"Were you trying to kill me too?" Rose asked through the locked door. "Was that what you had in mind when you told Tony Bick to kill my horse. That's what happened to my mothers horse, wasn't it? It didn't step in a gopher hole. You shot it, didn't you?"

"I couldn't let her get away and run off with that greaser!" he cried. "And I couldn't let you get away either. When I saw you riding off on that horse, it seemed like it was happening all over again. I had to stop you."

"Well, you stopped me," she said bitterly. "But I don't know what good you think it will do you. I can't stand the sight of you."

"By God," he said hoarsely, "I won't have you talking to me that way! I'm your father!"

"You're not man enough to be my father!" she said scornfully.

"If you don't start minding your tongue, I'm going to show you how much of a man I am!"

"Ha! Wouldn't you like to! I've known it all along!"

Hoffer bellowed like a stuck bull. "You twist everything I say! You think I've got a dirty mind, but you're the one who's got a dirty mind, or you wouldn't think such things! You're exactly like your mother!"

Rose was silent, as if frightened by his rage, or shocked by what he had said.

Whitey Cruger came out of the general store and stepped off the porch near his horse tied at the rail. Then he stopped in his tracks, his glazed bloodshot eyes going across the street to the corner of the last building. Whitey tensed and stood there like a lean hungry wolf, bristling and baring his teeth at what he saw.

What he saw was a tall man with a neatly trimmed chestnut beard and cold blue eyes. The man wore a ragged coat and a gun in a holster tied to his right leg. He stood there without moving or speaking and watched Whitey.

Stacy came out on the store porch and started to say something to Whitey. Then he too stopped suddenly and stared at the red-bearded man. His mouth fell open and he stepped quickly back into the store, rubbing his eyes as though he could not believe what he had seen.

Whitey Cruger had a small package in his left hand. He thrust the package into a pocket and with that same hand untied the reins without taking his eyes off the tall man. He turned the horse so that he could watch the man over the saddle as he mounted up.

The tall man stepped out away from the building, watching him steadily.

When he was in the saddle Whitey started walking his horse north along the street away from the tall man, but turned his head to keep an eye on him. The tall man did not move.

Then Whitey Cruger made a fatal mistake. He pulled his horse around and rode slowly back along the street. He could not bring himself to go the wrong way in order to avoid the man. He bent his white head to one side and his bloodshot eyes glittered with hatred as he drew near the man. The latter continued to watch him, still silent and somehow deadly.

Whitey started to ride on by, aware of the empty blue eyes watching him from the shadow of the hatbrim.

Then Whitey snarled and jerked out his gun.

The tall man's gun came up and bucked in his fist, and Whitey Cruger slumped sideways in the saddle. He dropped his own gun and grabbed for the horn, but missed it and tumbled to the ground. The horse stopped and stood nervously waiting for him to get back on. But Whitey Cruger would never ride again.

When Boyle and Stacy came out on the porch that was all they saw, the horse standing there in the street and Whitey Cruger lying dead on the ground. The tall man in the ragged coat had disappeared.

"Did you get a look at who killed him?" Boyle asked, shivering in the cold.

Stacy rubbed his eyes. "I ain't sure," he said, glancing toward the corner of the building where the red-bearded man had stood. "I think my eyes is goin' bad like Whitey's was. Must be some kind of eye trouble goin' around."

"If there is I sure hope it ain't catchin'," Boyle said before he thought.

A short time later Stacy was plodding south on a rented horse, with a message to deliver. Bad news, Mr. Hoffer. Another one of your men has been killed in town. Whitey Cruger this time.

Cruger's horse was now being given the royal treatment at the livery stable, for it was a Crown horse. It might be needed later to take Whitey out to the ranch, but more than likely Stacy would have to go back and dig him a grave next to those he had dug for Skip Leggett and Cal Whitty. Boyle took care of the undertaking business in town, with Stacy doing most of the work. Stacy glanced at the blisters on his hands and sighed. I'm going to ask for a raise if this keeps up, he thought.

He rode with is eyes on the ground, not paying much attention to the bleak empty desert about him, the buttes and rock formations that were slowly being carved by the restless, mournful wind. He was almost to the ranch when he suddenly looked up to find the tall red-bearded man sitting a lean, tough-looking horse in the trail before him.

Stacy halted the livery nag in its tracks and stared at the tall man in surprise. Few men frightened Stacy. Even Hayden had not frightened him, partly because it was so obvious that Hayden did not consider him worth bothering about. But now Stacy was frightened, for somehow he knew this man would kill him if he was not very careful. He could see it in those remote empty blue eyes that watched him as though he were dead already.

Stacy also knew with bleak certainty that he had wasted another long ride. The tall red-bearded man had no intention of moving aside and letting him continue his journey to the Crown Ranch.

"If you see Hoffer," Stacy said, sounding a little breathless, "tell him I'll go ahead and bury Whitey Cruger for him."

The tall man gazed back at him in silence, but Stacy thought he saw a faint gleam of humor in those bleak cold eyes. It did not reassure him, and he doubted if it was intended to.

"Well, I'll be seeing you," Stacy said, and pulled the horse around, looking over his shoulder with scared eyes as he headed back for town.

CHAPTER 10

Hayden and Mead started out shortly after breakfast, Hayden riding the tired black stallion, Mead on Hayden's bay gelding. Mead carried the double barrel shotgun in his hand. Hayden had his Winchester in his scabbard. He had shifted his own saddle to the black, giving Mead the saddle he had picked up last night at the Crown Ranch. It was not much, but Mead seemed happy with it. He was as excited as a city boy setting out on his first deer hunt in the country, and still seemed unaware of the fact that he himself would be hunted by men with guns who could shoot a lot better than he could and would not hesitate to kill him.

He had observed that Hayden's pale eyes were always half shut in the sunlight and wind, and he had started squinting his own eyes, and even tried to ride like the big man. At that did not succeed very well, but at least he managed to stay in the saddle and he guessed that was the main thing.

"Have you got a plan?" Mead asked finally, and smiled when Hayden glanced at him.

Hayden did not smile. "What I've got in mind I could do better alone," he said bluntly. "But if a man makes up his mind to commit suicide, there ain't much point in trying to stop him. And if you get yourself killed while you're with me, maybe I can get the ones who did it, if you don't get me killed too. That's what I'm worried about."

Mead could not think of anything else to say, so he laid the shotgun across the saddle in front of him and said nothing. In silence he followed Hayden up the steep trail to the top of the mesa, and then he gazed about with interest. It looked different in the daylight.

He soon realized that they were headed for the old Martin shack where they had stopped last night.

When they were still a half mile from the shack, Hayden reined in to study the layout with his sharp narrow eyes, the wind blowing the bleached grass and tugging at his hatbrim.

"Think Hoffer's men are there?" Mead asked.

"I don't see any sign of them."

They rode on in slowly, and without saying anything Hayden got down and unsaddled the black stallion and turned him into the corral. Mead started to put the bay in with him, but Hayden silently took the reins from him and put the gelding in the adjoining corral. Until then Mead had not noticed the partition between the two corrals.

Hayden put his saddle in the shed, but took his saddlebags, blanket roll, canteen and rifle into the shack. Mead followed with the shotgun and the blankets, extra clothing and sandwiches Helen had made him bring along.

At the door he stopped. It was the first time he had seen the inside of the shack. Hayden had cleaned up the mess Hoffer's men had made, but the place could still use a good cleaning, something it evidently had not known in a long time.

Mead noticed that Hayden had put his stuff down and was brushing the dust from a black suit that hung from a nail in the wall.

"That's not a bad looking suit."

"It was Frank's," Hayden said. "I bought it for him. He was saving it to be buried in. I think he had a feeling he would be killed."

"Looks like he didn't get his wish. About being buried in the suit, I mean."

"Looks that way."

"What was he like?" Mead asked curiously.

Hayden thought for a moment. "It's hard to say what he was like. He had the original poker face and he never had much to say, so it was hard to tell what he had on his mind."

Mead glanced about the nearly empty room. "He didn't have much furniture, did he?"

"His bedroll was his furniture," Hayden replied. "He was a mustanger."

"Where is his bedroll?" Mead asked.

"I've been wondering about that. I've been wondering about a lot of things that don't add up."

Hayden spread his blankets on the floor against the wall and lay down on them, removing nothing but his sheepskin coat. "Since you're here, you might as well make yourself useful," he said. "Keep watch and wake me up if you see anyone."

"You going to sleep?" Mead asked.

"That's the general idea," Hayden answered, and pulled his black hat down over his eyes. "I didn't get much last night."

The Crown riders halted below the west wall of the mesa and sat their horses for a long time without moving or speaking, looking up at the rim.

Then Tony Bick nudged his animal forward. "Let's go."

Hoke Kelsey scowled. "What if he's up there?"

"If he is," Tony Bick replied, "he'll kill me first. Then maybe the rest of you yellow bellies can get away before he gets you. He might even let you go, if you don't pile up and trample each other to death coming down that cliff. I'm sure he'd enjoy watching that."

"Ain't none of us yaller," Hoke snarled. "We just got stampeded yesterday. It won't happen again."

Tony Bick looked at him through cold eyes. "If it does," he said, "Hayden won't have to kill you. I'll do it myself."

"You better make the first one count," Hoke Kelsey told him, "'cause that's all you'll get."

"I always make the first one count," Bick said.

They went up the steep trail single file, Tony Bick in the lead, Kelsey behind him, the others spread out about ten feet apart. The cold wind hit them in the face when they reached the rim, but there was no sign of Hayden, just some tracks on the ground.

"That's stallion's tracks turned south," Kelsey said. "Looks like he didn't go back to that old shack."

Tony Bick sat his horse looking east across the mesa. "I figure he just rode around in circles for a while leaving a long trail to wear out our horses, and then went back to the shack. But I could be wrong."

Kelsey was still scowling at the ground. "There's some tracks here I ain't seen before."

Tony Bick did not even glance at the ground. "I've seen them before. That greenhorn's with him."

Hoke Kelsey's mouth fell open in astonishment. "The hell you say! What's he want to saddle hisself with a greenhorn for, at a time like this?"

Bick grinned. "Maybe Hayden's trying to get him killed so he can have his woman. She ain't bad looking. Face ain't nothing to brag about, but if she had some decent clothes the rest wouldn't be bad at all."

"If Mead's with Hayden," one of the younger men said with a dirty grin, "why don't we go over there and pay her a little visit?"

"We'll pay her a little visit after we get them two," Bick said, putting his horse in motion. "Some of us will," he added. "The ones who're left."

Hayden woke up about noon, yawning and stretching. Mead stood at the window, eating one of the sandwiches he had brought.

"Seen anything?" Hayden asked.

Mead looked out the window. "Nothing yet."

Hayden sat up, grinning. "When they find out you're with me, they may be afraid to come around."

Mead smiled also, but said nothing. He knew it was meant as a joke.

"One of them sandwiches wouldn't go bad about now," Hayden remarked.

Mead took him a sandwich, then returned to the window.

"A pot of hot coffee wouldn't go bad either," Hayden added. "But I guess there ain't no use asking for trouble."

"You think they might see the smoke?"

"I wouldn't put it past them."

Hayden ate the sandwich in a few bites, then carefully rolled and tied his blankets.

Mead watched with interest. "You going to leave soon."

"I just want to be ready in case I have to," Hayden said. "It always pays a man to be ready."

"If we're going to stay here a while," Mead said, "shouldn't we bring in plenty of water?"

Hayden's eyes brightened but seemed colder. "That's a good idea. Why don't you trot down to the waterhole and fill that bucket and that old keg you were sitting on when you were supposed to be keeping watch."

Mead flushed. "How did you know?"

"I woke up a time or two and saw you sitting there fooling with that old pistol instead of keeping your eyes peeled."

"Why didn't you say anything?"

"I needed to get some sleep, and I knew if I got myself awake enough to get after you I wouldn't be able to go back to sleep. Besides," he added, "I don't figure Hoffer's men will get too close in the daylight."

Mead was silent a moment, looking out the window. Then he said, "I didn't figure you'd come here. These walls look pretty thin and rotten. They won't stop bullets, will they?"

"Not likely," Hayden agreed. "But I'm afraid they may take a notion to burn this place down whether we're here or not, and I'd like to make it as costly for them as I can."

"I see," Mead said. "I guess I better get that water. We may need it."

He stood the shotgun against the wall and bent down to lift the keg. Then he stopped. "There's some water in it."

"I imagine it's getting pretty stale by now. Why don't you dump it in that trough at the corral."

"I don't believe I noticed it. Is it inside the corral?"

"Half inside and half out. Half in one corral and half in the other. So you won't have to get close to that stallion. That's one reason I decided to come here. That devil won't give us much trouble as long as he's in that corral. No way he can get out of there without some help."

"He won't get it from me," Mead said. "I feel a lot better with a high fence between me and that horse."

He took the keg out and soon brought it back filled.

Hayden was sitting on the floor with his back against the wall. He grinned at Mead and said, "That wasn't hard, was it? You're right husky for an invalid."

"I'm not exactly an invalid," Mead grunted, as he eased the keg to the floor.

"I didn't figure there was much wrong with you except laziness," Hayden responded. "You should be ashamed of yourself, letting your wife take care of you."

Mead made no reply until he had filled the bucket. Then he resumed his position at the window with the shotgun. After a moment he glanced at Hayden out of the corner of his eye and said in a cautious tone, "When I met Helen she was working at that restaurant. I went there nearly every evening for about a week, but she never seemed to pay any attention to me. I noticed that she never said more than a few words to men who looked strong and healthy. But when some old man came in all bent over and looking half dead, then she'd hurry over with a glass of water and make a fuss over him. So one evening I went in all stopped over and coughing my head off, and she kept coming over to see if there was anything she could get me. I think that was the first time she ever noticed me, because she didn't seem to remember that I'd been in before.

"I told her there was something wrong with my lungs, but the doctors didn't know what it was or how to cure it. I saw this look come into her eyes, like she felt so sorry for me it nearly broke her heart. I kept going there and she always came over to talk to me. Well, after a while we got married. I think she only married me so she'd have someone to take care of, and I was afraid she'd leave me if she found out there wasn't really anything wrong with me."

Hayden laughed, and then thought over what Mead had said. "Well, I guess it ain't all your fault then. I don't rightly blame you for trying to be what she wanted. There've been times when I found myself trying to behave like a gentleman because that was what some girl seemed to expect."

"I can't picture you behaving like a gentleman," Mead said.

"I said I tried to behave like one. I didn't say I was any good at it. Anybody who aims to be a gentleman or a gunfighter should get a early start. Me and you both waited too late."

"I don't know," Mead said slowly. "I've been practicing a little. I think I could soon learn how to draw pretty fast."

"Being fast on the draw won't do you much good if you can't hit the broad side of a barn," Hayden told him. "When Hoffer's men come at us you better use that scattergun and save that old pistol till they get so close you can reach out and club them over the head with it. That's the only way you'll hit them with it."

He scowled. "Speaking of Hoffer's men—you keep standing there at that window. What makes you think they'll come that way? They may circle around behind that rocky hill south of us."

"I don't guess it would hurt you to take a look now and then," Mead said. "You keep talking about me being lazy, but I notice you ain't doing too much. You slept half the morning, and now you're just sitting there hugging your knees."

Hayden groaned softly and rubbed his eyes. "After wrestling with that stallion the biggest part of the night, I don't even feel like sitting up, much less doing anything. I must be getting old. I can remember when it didn't bother me that much. But I ain't tangled with many like him."

He grinned. "I need nursing more than you do."

Mead shrugged. "Well, if I get myself killed, I'm sure Helen would be glad to take care of you. But it might help if you went in there all shot up and bleeding all over the place."

"It may come to that." Hayden climbed wearily to his feet and checked his guns. "But I'd just as soon stay healthy, if I can. I never could figure out what good a sick or hurt man would be to a woman. But then I never could figure out what most women see in the men they take up with."

Mead glanced at him. "Like me, for instance?"

"I don't think I'd consider you much of a catch if I was a woman. But I don't guess the problem will ever come up."

Hayden stepped to the south window with his rifle and peered at the boulder-strewn hill that had been worrying him. He saw no sign of Hoffer's men, but he had not expected to this soon.

He circled the large room, pausing at each window to peer out. Except for the window where Mead was, all the windows were small and had no glass in them. They had been covered with pieces of canvas before Hayden removed them the night of his return.

"If they come at us from that side," he said, "knock that glass out the first thing, or you may find yourself picking it out of your face. Too bad your wife ain't here to do it for you."

"It's going to get mighty cold in here about tonight," Mead said, shivering at the thought.

"It sure is," Hayden agreed. "Before this is over you may wish you'd stayed at home where you belong." After a moment he added, "But Hoffer's men may make it nice and warm for us. They may burn this place down around our ears."

CHAPTER 11

The Crown riders followed the stallion's tracks almost to the south end of the mesa before the trail suddenly curved around to the north.

"That's what I figured he'd do," Tony Bick said. "But it don't matter. He won't be able to see us as well when it gets dark."

"I wondered why you was takin' your time," Hoke Kelsey growled.

"You think he's gone back to that old shack?" another man asked.

Bick nodded, looking north across the bleak gray mesa. "There's a good stout corral there for that stallion, and a waterhole right in front of the house. I figure he'll stay there as long as he can."

When it was getting dark in the shack on the mesa, Hayden opened a can of tomatoes and handed it to Mead. Then he opened a can for himself and speared out the tomatoes with his knife, afterwards drinking the cold juice from the can. He had left a sack of grub at the Mead shack, but there was still enough food here to last him and Mead several days. He figured that was longer than they would last. He shook his head and told himself he would last longer if Mead was up there with Hoffer's men, spreading chaos and confusion among them. A greenhorn like Mead could help his own side more by trying to help the enemy.

"I've still got a sandwich left," Mead said.

"Save it," Hayden said, his hard face unreadable. "You may get hungry on that long cold watch after midnight."

After a little silence, Mead asked, "How many men has Hoffer got?"

"I think he usually keeps only ten or twelve during the winter."

"That's enough, ain't it?" Mead asked.

"It's not as many as he has in the summer. But he usually keeps his meanest and toughest hands. They don't do much work in the winter. Hoffer only keeps them to frighten greenhorns and squatters and stock thieves off his range."

Mead set the empty can on the floor, then glanced at Hayden in the deepening gloom and said, "What does Hoffer want with so much land? He must not have very many cows. I don't think I've seen but two or three in all, and I've made three trips across his range going to town."

"I don't think he brought a very big herd here from Texas, and he sold some. But he's thinking of the future. He wants to stake his claim on the whole country because it takes about twenty acres of range like this to fatten one cow. And a man like Hoffer just naturally wants everything for himself."

Hayden drained the last of the juice from the tomato can and reached for his rifle, stepping to the door. "I'm going to take a look around. If there's anything in your can, don't leave it there where you'll kick it over in the dark."

He took his own can outside and set it on the ground not far from the shack. If Hoffer's men tried to creep up in the dark, maybe one of them would blunder into the can. It was unlikely that Mead would see them, if he was on watch.

They had fed and watered the horses before dark, giving them a little grain and wild hay from the shed and filling the trough with water from the waterhole. The stallion was rested and restless, circling the corral, seeking a way out. Hayden's bay looked over the bars of the adjacent corral and nickered softly. Hayden answered with a quiet word. He knew it would be pointless to try to quiet the wild-eyed stallion down, so he did not try.

It was full dark now. There was no moon, no stars were visible. He held the Winchester lightly in his hands and looked toward the isolated, boulder-strewn hill to the south. It almost seemed to be creeping closer in the darkness, the ancient friend of attackers and lawless men. Hayden knew the hill was more than two hundred yards away, but even at that distance a man with a good rifle could stand up in those rocks and make it very uncomfortable for those in the shack, for the half-rotted plank walls would not stop bullets. Eight or ten men with rifles could soon turn the shack into a sieve.

Yet Hayden was reluctant to leave. An old streak of stubbornness had asserted itself. Hoffer's men had tried to drive Frank Martin off and then had shot him when he resisted. Hayden had made up his mind to give them the same chance at him. He had not spent as much time here as Martin had, but he had come to think of the place as home, and if they tried to run him off they would have a fight on their hands.

He warily circled the shack, but saw nothing. For a short time he stood looking west across the mesa, the wind chilling him to the bone. Then he went back inside.

"What did you do with your can?" Mead asked.

"Put it out there where maybe they'll step on it and wake you up if you go to sleep on your watch."

"I might as well take mine out. It's empty."

"Better let me do it. Then I'll know where it is. I don't want to walk into it in the dark when I go outside."

Hayden had just stepped back outside when the riders suddenly appeared, circling the shack in a line and yelling like Comanches. They were bent low over the necks of their horses to make smaller targets and moving sideways in front of him, about thirty yards away. It made for difficult shooting in the dark, and perhaps he should have realized at once that their goal was to get him to waste his lead. But the only thought in his mind was that they had come to kill him or drive him off. He dropped the can and began firing in a cold rage, working the lever of his Winchester and ignoring the bullets that smacked into the wall behind him.

A horse went down, but the rider stood up blazing away with a six-shooter. Hayden nailed him with two quick shots and shifted his rifle to a new target.

The shotgun blasted through the shack window and glass rained like hail around him.

"What are you doing?" he howled over his shoulder.

"I forgot," Mead apologized.

"Knock that glass out, you fool! Use the other end of that scatter-gun! And watch where you shoot! You'll hit me!"

He levered a shell into the Winchester, but the riders were gone, racing for the rocky hill, leaving one dead man and one dead horse behind. Hayden emptied his rifle after them, but without effect. They disappeared in the brush and boulders at the foot of the slope.

Hayden stood in the yard and reloaded his Winchester with cartridges from the loops on his belt. The rifle used the same .44 cartridges as his Colts.

Mead was knocking the glass out of the window with the butt of the shotgun. The sound irritated Hayden, but he kept his irritation to himself. After all, that was what he had told Mead to do.

He was just as irritated with himself for bringing the greenhorn along. He should have known better. But he had not expected to get his back full of glass and buckshot, which he had just missed doing.

As he turned to go back inside he saw the empty tomato can he had dropped, and gave it an angry kick out of his way. The can bounced and rolled noisily until it stopped in the dead weeds near the house.

Inside, he got a box of cartridges from his saddlebag and filled all the loops in his gun belt, then emptied the rest of the cartridges into a coat pocket. There was another box of cartridges in the saddlebag, but if he was not more careful with his ammunition he would probably run out before this was over. Wild shooting in the dark would soon exhaust an ammunition factory.

A bullet splintered the south wall and whistled past Hayden. He swore under his breath and heard Mead dive to the floor, dropping the shotgun. It clattered on the boards but did not go off as Hayden had feared, so it probably wasn't cocked.

"Try to take care of that old shotgun," Hayden told the greenhorn. "I didn't give it to you. I just loaned it to you. I want it back when this is over. I want to keep it because it belonged to Frank."

Mead scarcely seemed to hear him. He was lying flat on his belly but had his head raised peering about in the dark. He jerked his head back down when another bullet tore through the wall. It was followed by a whole volley that buzzed at the shack like angry hornets shot from guns. The guns popped and roared from the hill amid scattered jeers and catcalls. This time Hayden hit the floor, gripping his Winchester and wishing he was up there among them, using the rifle like a club.

When there was a lull in the shooting, Mead wondered aloud, "Why did anybody build a house this close to that hill?"

"I wasn't here then," Hayden said, "but I imagine that waterhole had something to do with it. Good water is mighty hard to find in this country. The only other water on the mesa is a bad-tasting spring that's dry about half of the time. I don't know how Hoffer plans to raise cows up here, unless he aims to bring in well diggers and wind-mills."

"Speaking of water, I feel awful damp for some reason."

"You didn't!"

"No, I didn't. It's the keg. There's a hole in it and the water's pour-ing out all over me!"

"Then you better find yourself another spot," Hayden told him.

"I guess a bullet hit it," Mead said as he moved away from the keg.

"Seems likely," Hayden said. "You'll have something to cough about if you come down with the flu. But it might cure you of pretend-ing to be sick when you ain't."

"You think I ought to change clothes?" Mead asked as though alarmed at the prospect of actually getting sick. "I brought some with me."

"I think I'd wait a bit if it was me, until we see what they're going to do," Hayden advised. "There will soon be water all over the floor, and the other clothes would soon get wet too."

"My blankets!" Mead cried, scrambling to snatch them away from the leaky water keg. "They're already wet! And my extra clothes are wrapped up inside the blankets!"

"Looks like a cold wet night, don't it?" Hayden commented, grin-ning in the dark. Perversely, he was amused at Mead's alarm. "Don't worry about it," he added in a reassuring tone. "You probably won't live long enough to take the flu."

Mead responded with unexpected anger. "Thanks, Hayden. You're a real cheerful cuss at times."

"I see you've got a temper," Hayden said, still grinning. "But you better save it for Hoffer's men. I'm on your side, remember?"

"I'm not so sure about that," Mead retorted, wringing water from his blankets as though it were a neck he was wringing—perhaps Hayden's. "I've been thinking about it all day. I half believe both you and Helen want to get me killed so you and her can team up."

"I thought you said she didn't like big strong men."

"I never said she didn't like them. I said she didn't have anything much to do with them. But when they ain't noticing, I've seen her look at big husky lunks with a sort of dreamy look in her eyes. And I think she's tired of taking care of me. I think she wants someone who can take care of her and protect her from men like Hoffer's bunch. That's one reason I want to learn how to shoot. It burns me up every time I think about the way they talked to her and looked at her right in front of me, and I just stood there, afraid to say anything."

"And here I was thinking it didn't bother you to hide behind her skirts and let her take care of you."

"It bothers me a lot. I just wish I knew what she really wants, someone she can take care of or someone who can take care of her."

"Maybe it works both ways," Hayden suggested.

Mead started to say something, then turned his head toward the sound of more bullets hitting the plank wall and guns popping on the hill.

"Better stay down," Hayden said in a quiet, bleak tone. "Looks like they hope to get us with a lucky shot. They know that wall wouldn't stop an angry hornet."

"That's what those bullets sound like," Mead said. "But they've quit yelling. What do you think that means?"

"I guess they just got tired of it. Maybe their throats got raw from yelling in that cold wind."

Mead glanced at the gaping window and shivered in his wet clothes. "I wish now I hadn't knocked that glass out."

"Them clothes in that blanket roll may not be wet," Hayden said. "A good blanket will turn a lot of water."

"They'd soon get wet on me. I'm laying in a puddle of water."

"You might consider moving out of it," Hayden grated. "And if that keg's still leaking you could set it outside till it stops. I figure it's about as safe out there as it is in here."

"I think it's about quit leaking now. It's already leaked down to the bullet hole."

"I guess there ain't much use in putting it outside then."

"Guess not," Mead agreed. "Looks like filling that keg wasn't such a good idea."

"It was a good idea all right. The water that's left in that keg may come in handy."

"I could use a drink, but the dipper's in the bucket on that shelf," Mead said. "My mouth's the only thing that's dry, and it's the only thing I wish was wet."

"Go ahead and get a drink. The shooting's stopped and it may be a while before they open up again."

"I believe I'll wait a little."

"Suit yourself."

It was a long wait. Mead lay motionless on his belly with his elbows braced under him, holding his head and the shotgun up off the wet floor. Hayden, now sitting with his back to the wall and his Winchester across his knees, watched in amazement, wondering how long Mead could maintain that awkward position.

After a while Hayden shook his head and bit off the end of a cigar. It would be a great comfort to have Frank Martin here instead of a greenhorn, but it looked like he would have to do the best he could without Frank. When he lit the cigar, Mead glanced around at him.

"You don't smoke, do you, Mead?"

Mead shook his head. "I used to, but Helen said it was bad for my lungs." He sounded embarrassed. "She said she'd marry me if I quit smoking, and she wouldn't marry me till I did. It took me quite a while to decide which one would be the hardest to do without."

Hayden laughed quietly. "I think you made the right choice. But if a woman couldn't take me the way I am, I think I'd just stick to horses and cigars."

"And guns?" Mead asked.

Hayden nodded. "When they're needed."

Mead smiled in the dark and was silent. Apparently he had forgotten that his clothes were wet and his mouth was dry.

After watching him in silence for a while, Hayden asked, "Did you reload that shotgun after nearly filling my back full of glass and buckshot?"

Mead lay silent and seemed to be trying to remember.

"You didn't, did you?" Hayden growled. "All this time you've had your thumb on the hammers of that scattergun, ready to cock it and blast away. But that scattergun is empty. If I hadn't thought to ask you, it would still be empty when you need the thing, and while you were trying to figure out why it just clicked when you pulled the trigger, Hoffer's men would be smiling and filling you full of holes."

Too embarrassed to reply Mead broke the shotgun open to replace the two empty shells.

At that moment one of the empty tomato cans rattled outside the shack.

CHAPTER 12

Hayden came up off the floor like a big cat, heard the hiss of his cigar as he dropped it in the water bucket and the pounding of a man's boots as he leaped to the window. The man vanished like a shadow in the darkness. Yet in that one fleeting glimpse Hayden had seen enough to know that the man was short, bowlegged, and very fast on his feet.

Mead was making curious motions to rise. Hayden pushed him back down, stepped over him and shoved the door open, leaping out into the night.

The running man was now almost to the arroyo that headed just below the waterhole and angled southeast around the foot of the rocky hill where Hoffer's men were. It seemed incredible but Hayden had somehow forgotten about that arroyo. He raised his rifle and levered two shots, but the man, apparently unhurt, leaped astride a horse waiting in the arroyo and galloped away, disappearing behind a scrubby fringe of brush where the arroyo deepened.

Knowing it was hopeless, Hayden abandoned the chase and walked back toward the shack as Hoffer's men began firing from the cone-shaped hill. Hayden ignored the whistling bullets and glared in amazement as Mead appeared at the door with the bucket and threw the water out.

"Hey, what's the idea?" the big man asked.

"I don't like your cigars, Hayden," Mead said. "I think you should try a different brand or keep them out of the drinking water."

It was the young hand called Shorty who had volunteered to sneak up
to the shack, poke his gun in through the window and blast Hayden
and the greenhorn before they knew what hit them.

Shorty was embarrassed when he got back to the cold windy hill
and had to explain his failure to an unsmiling Tony Bick. Tony had
all but quit smiling. The bungling incompetence and cross-grained
stupidity of most of the hands, once so amusing, had rapidly palled
when he was given the job of leading them on a dangerous manhunt,
and their stubborn refusal to straighten out had begun to erode his
sense of humor. That was what responsibility did to a man, Shorty
thought. It made him fault-finding and hard to live with. But now
they all blamed Shorty. He could see them there on the dark rocky
hill, scowling at him in silent scorn.

"What happened?" Bick demanded, his voice hoarse from yelling
taunts at Hayden and orders at the Crown men.

Shorty's bowlegs wobbled nervously when he spoke. He usually
tried to get on high ground so he would not have to look up at the one
he was talking to, but Tony Bick towered there on the rough slope
above him, looking even taller than he was.

"Hayden had tin cans scattered all over the place. I got past all of
them but one—"

"Don't lie to me," Bick snapped. "There wasn't any cans lyin'
around the other day when I was down there, and Hayden hasn't
had time to empty many since he got back. The one you stepped on
was prob'ly the only one down there. Then when Hayden came out
you could of nailed him easy, but you lost your nerve and ran like a
jackrabbit."

Shorty's bowlegs wobbled frantically. He wanted desperately to
run now—from Tony Bick. He could not think of a single thing to
say in his defense. Nothing that would convince Bick, anyway. More
lame excuses would only enrage him.

"I guess you heard what Hoffer told me to do if anybody ran?"
Bick asked.

Shorty gasped and rolled his eyes in terror.

"I should put a bullet in you," Bick said, already turning away in
disgust. "But you ain't worth a bullet. I may need it for Hayden. From
now on your job is taking care of the horses and running errands.
That's all you're fit for."

Shorty almost wept with relief. There for a moment he had felt sure Tony Bick would kill him, and he might do so yet if Shorty displeased him in any way. It seemed that Bick could not go for long without killing someone, and if they did not soon get Hayden, Shorty might well become his next victim.

But if Shorty could redeem himself in some way, maybe by killing Hayden or that greenhorn—and actually getting the job done this time—then perhaps Bick would turn his gun on someone else.

An idea suddenly occurred to Shorty. But he decided to say nothing this time. Bick might think him unequal to the task and refuse to let him go. Well, this time Shorty would act first and talk later. He would show them.

He saw that Bick and the others had already forgotten him and turned their attention back to the shack. Just as well. That would make it easier for Shorty to slip away unnoticed. He turned and angled down the steep slope, making his way silently through the brush and boulders. He had heard that mesas were flat on top, but this one was anything but flat. Well, it was flat in places, but elsewhere there were ridges and valleys and isolated buttes just like on the desert below. And the scrubby sage that grew almost everywhere, he had found out, was not really sage at all, but some other kind of shrub. But around here anything that resembled sage was called sage.

He unsaddled his horse and staked it near the others on some dry grass. This time he would go on foot. There would be less likelihood of being detected. Hayden would be more alert this time, so he would have to be careful.

Descending the steep bank, he made his way rapidly along the arroyo, confident that he would not be seen or heard. His boots made almost no sound in the deep sand, and brush fringed the rim of the arroyo, concealing him even from the Crown men on the slope above him. His size also helped—he was not much over five feet tall, but wiry and strong. He had repeatedly demonstrated that he had as much stamina as any of the men on the ranch, and to prove himself their equal he was willing to take risks that they were not. Had he not already proved that once tonight? If only that can had not been hidden in the weeds right in his path, as if Hayden had known that was the way he would come ...

Those tall dead weeds were on Shorty's mind now as he neared his destination. They had concealed that can from him, but now he could pay them and Hayden back at the same time.

Some rank dry grass grew on one side of the arroyo. Shorty bent down and tore off a handful, twisted it into a tight ball and tied a pigging string around it. Then he reached into his pocket for a match. Hayden would rush out to fight the blaze, and this time Shorty, hidden safely in the arroyo, would nail him.

Even in the dark it was apparent that the adventure was already beginning to pall on Mead. He no longer suffered Hayden's instructive abuse as his due, and at times without warning he made a cutting remark of his own. He found things to complain about. A side of his nature had surfaced that intrigued Hayden.

It just might be, the big mustanger thought, that I had this greenhorn pegged wrong. He ain't quite the fool I thought he was.

But in a man like Mead a brain could be a drawback, especially if he tried to use it. It would be a lot simpler if he let Hayden do the thinking for both of them.

But Mead did not see it that way. He seemed convinced that Hayden, out of pure cussedness, was deliberately making things hard for him, and quite possibly trying to get him killed.

As for Hayden, he was afraid Mead would get them both killed without trying.

Mead had unrolled his blankets to examine the clothes inside. "Soaking wet," he said, aiming an accusing look at Hayden in the dark. Hayden did not know so much after all, the look seemed to say.

"I guess they ain't as waterproof as they looked," Hayden commented, reaching for another cigar, but not lighting it.

"There's nothing wrong with the blankets," Mead said. "This is the first time I've heard blankets were supposed to be waterproof."

"Some are and some ain't," Hayden said. "You ever see one of them blanket ponchos like the Mexicans wear? They're nearly as good as a slicker, and a lot less trouble."

"What's a slicker?"

"Raincoat."

"I had a good raincoat," Mead said, wringing the extra shirt he had brought, "but somebody stole it."

"When was this?"

"Before we left Chicago. I hung it up in the restaurant one night and when I started to leave it was gone."

"Not many sneak thieves out here," Hayden said. "But somebody might stick a gun in your face and cart off your money."

"They wouldn't need a cart," Mead said. "They could carry all I've got in their watch pocket, and still have plenty of room for the watch."

"Sounds like we're in about the same boat," Hayden replied, glancing through the small east window. "This time I came back about like I left. I had a little over two hundred dollars saved up, but the night before I started back I got a notion to build it up to two or three thousand in a poker game. It was wishful thinking. Cardsharp cleaned me out, and I never even managed to spot how he did it."

"Maybe he wasn't even cheating. Maybe you're just not as good as you thought."

Hayden heard the quiet malice in Mead's tone and glanced at him in irritation. "Looks like this here game has gone sour for you," he grunted. "You thought it would be all riding and shooting. You never expected to be hugging a wet floor on a cold windy night while men you can't even see shoot bullets through the wall."

"If you ask me, we shouldn't have come here in the first place," Mead said.

"Where should we have gone?"

"I don't know, but not here." Then he said, "Maybe up there on that hill where Hoffer's men are."

"I thought about it," Hayden said. "But I figured they'd come here first, and I wanted to be here to greet them."

"Well, you greeted them all right," Mead said. "But they'll be back."

Hayden was still looking out the small window hole. He stared in amazement as a ball of flame arced through the darkness and landed in the tall dead weeds not ten feet from the shack. A bright blaze shot up almost immediately.

"It looks like they're back already!" he exclaimed as he jerked up his Winchester.

He looked beyond the blaze in the yard and saw the man at the lip of the arroyo drawing back his hand to hurl another ball of burning grass. Hayden fired in the same instant. The man cried out in pain and surprise and fell backward into the arroyo, the burning missile still in his hand.

Hayden put his rifle down, leaped to the water keg, wrenched the lid off and grabbed one of Mead's blankets, stuffing it down into the keg.

"Hey!" Mead cried hoarsely. "That's my blanket! And it's wet enough already!"

"Grab the other one and come on!" Hayden snarled. "We've got a fire to fight!"

He flung the door open and ran toward the blazing, crackling weeds. The wind was whipping the blaze toward the shack.

When the flame leaped up near the shack, Tony Bick rose to peer over his boulder. He had given no orders to fire the shack. "Who's that down there?" he demanded in a tone of outrage.

"It ain't me," Hoke Kelsey grunted. Then he grinned—and Hoke Kelsey had not grinned since the last time he told about skinning a Comanche alive down on the Rio Grande. "But it ain't such a bad idea."

"That old shack might come in handy when Hoffer has us herding cattle on this mesa," Bick said.

"I hadn't thought of that."

As Kelsey spoke, a rifle roared from the shack window. A moment later a tall man ran out with a blanket and began slapping it furiously at the blaze. He looked like a dark giant outlined against the fire.

"Now's our chance!' Kelsey said, bringing up his rifle.

"Let him put the fire out first," Tony Bick snapped, then spoke sharply to the other dark shapes crouched behind boulders along the slope. "Hold your fire!"

The Crown men reluctantly obeyed, muttering to themselves as they lowered their rifles.

Tony Bick had borrowed the cook's rifle. He did not have one of his own.

"Who's missing?" he asked. "Who's down there?"

"It ain't me," someone grumbled, echoing Kelsey.

"It ain't me neither," someone else said.

Bick suddenly glanced over his shoulder, then glared down toward the bottom of the rocky slope where the horses were picketed. "Where's Shorty?"

"I figure that's him down there," Hoke said, grinning again. He had never liked small men. "I guess Hayden kilt the little bastard."

"If he didn't," Bick said, "I will."

He turned his attention back to the scene below. Another man ran from the shack, also carrying a blanket. But the big man, flailing savagely, had already annihilated the blaze. He roared something over his shoulder and the other man ran back inside, to reappear a moment later with a bucket. He ran toward the waterhole to fill the bucket. The big man grabbed an old shovel—Bick had seen it the other day—and appeared to be digging a trench around the burned area.

"That must be Hayden," Hoke Kelsey said, no longer grinning. "Bastard don't scare easy, does he? I noticed when we was shootin' at him before he never even seemed to pay no attention. I saw him stop in the yard and stand there for about a minute talkin' to that greenhorn at the door."

"I guess by now he knows we can't hit nothin'!" Bick said bitterly. "I never used a rifle before, and it looks like the rest of you didn't either."

Shorty lay in the arroyo on his back, groaning. His right shoulder throbbed painfully, and he had fallen on a rock when he fell. The rock was still under his back, causing him almost as much discomfort as the bullet in his shoulder. But he was still too stunned to move, and he was almost afraid to move until he knew how badly he was hurt.

The bundle of grass had burned away in the sand only about two feet from his head, but doing no harm. It had not done any good either, Shorty thought sadly.

He discovered that he was still gripping his Winchester in his left hand. But it was no good to him now. He could not use his right hand and he could not manage the rifle with just his left. He could use his Colt, but not the Winchester. So he flung the rifle into the tall grass where he could get it later. No one was likely to spot it there if he had to leave it for a few days.

He heard feet running this way and he frantically reached over with his left hand to fumble the gun from his holster. Then the footsteps abruptly halted. He heard water sloshing in a bucket, heard the feet pounding back toward the shack. Then he remembered hearing Hayden bawl just a few moments before, "Get that bucket! You emptied it, now fill it back up and water this burnt ground!"

He soon heard the greenhorn running back down toward the waterhole, which was not more than twenty feet from where Shorty lay in the sandy arroyo. This was his chance, Shorty thought grimly. He could at least plug that greenhorn before he made tracks back to the hill, and if Hayden came after him, Shorty would wait for him in the darkness and plug him too.

Holding his right arm stiff against his side, Shorty pushed himself up with his left hand. Here the arroyo was less than five feet deep, so it was not necessary for Shorty to climb the bank to see what was going on. He could see Hayden up by the shack, digging and scraping with a shovel as if he had forgotten the riflemen on the hill. For a moment Shorty wondered why Bick and the others were not firing. Then he turned his attention to the waterhole where Mead was just rising back up with another bucket of water.

The heavy Colt felt awkward in Shorty's left hand, but he got the hammer back, steadied his hand on the ground, squinted along the dark barrel and squeezed the trigger.

It was a clean miss, but he almost smiled at the greenhorn's reaction. Mead dropped the bucket as though it had burst into flame, gaped in disbelief at Shorty's head sticking out of the arroyo, and then yelled hoarsely at Hayden, "He's still alive! He's shooting at me!"

"Then shoot back, you fool!" Hayden bellowed.

Mead had left the shotgun in the shack and he knew it would be a miracle if he hit anything with the old Starr pistol, but he grasped the wooden stock with a trembling hand and pulled the gun from the holster just as the man in the arroyo fired again. Flame leapt from the muzzle and the explosion almost scared him to death. His first wild impulse was to drop his own pistol and run for the shack. Then he became aware of two things at once. The bullet kicked up dust several feet away, and the man was shooting with his left hand. Obviously, he was too badly wounded to shoot with his right hand, and a very poor shot with his left. Mead himself could do no worse.

With savage delight, Mead ran toward the arroyo, raising the gun in his hand and blasting away at the man's head. The old Starr almost jumped out of his fist and its roar nearly burst his eardrums. But he was gratified to see the man ducking his head and then turning to run along the bottom of the arroyo. Mead leaped into the arroyo and ran after him.

The small bowlegged man whirled to fire at him, then ran on in frantic haste, groaning under his breath. Mead emptied his gun without hitting the bobbing target ahead, then slowed down to reload. The man disappeared around a curve in the arroyo, and then Mead heard Hayden bawling at him, "Come back here, you fool, before he kills you!"

Mead reluctantly turned back, and was still nervously fumbling cartridges into his gun when he approached the shack. "Why did you call me back?" he asked. "You ran after him before, didn't you?"

"Follow my advice, not my example," Hayden told him. "It's one thing for me to go chasing after somebody in the dark. It's something else for you to. It ain't like you know what you're doing out there, and you couldn't hit a bear from inside his belly with that old pistol. From now on you hold onto that scattergun, no matter what else you're carrying."

"In case you didn't know it, Hayden, there's no guarantee I would hit him with the shotgun," Mead answered. "I tried to get a couple of rabbits day before yesterday and I didn't come anywhere near them."

"That don't surprise me. Maybe you should of just run them down and hit them over the head with it."

Just then the rifles began roaring again from the rocky hill. Hayden glanced in that direction. "Maybe we better get back inside," he suggested. "Seems like they can't shoot much better than you, but one of them might get lucky."

The guns fell silent as Shorty made his way, gasping and groaning, up the steep rocky slope. They had spotted him, and were now up there watching him in an ominous silence that made his scalp prickle. But as he got closer he heard Hoke Kelsey ask what sounded like an idle question.

"Why ain't we down there in that arroyo instead of way off up here where we can't hit nothin'?"

"You ever had a face full of buckshot?" Tony Bick asked, keeping his eyes on Shorty. "They've got that scattergun down there. At that range all they'd have to do is point it toward that arroyo and pull the trigger."

"Not necessarily, if that greenhorn's usin' it," Hoke said. "Shorty's been down there twice, and he ain't got no face full of buckshot."

"He's got something," Tony Bick said, noticing the way Shorty was holding his right arm and shoulder. Then he asked, "Where's your rifle?"

Shorty stopped in his tracks and looked back down toward the shack. He did not answer. It was not necessary.

"I should send you back after it," Bick said. "But it don't look like you'll need it anymore. You weren't much good before, but you're worse than useless with a busted shoulder."

Shorty remained silent, except for his heavy breathing. He seemed afraid to look at Tony Bick, much less say anything.

"Who told you to go down there and burn that shack?" Bick asked in a rougher tone. "It may come in handy before long. And you might

of burned off this whole mesa, including this hill where we're standing. I don't think Hoffer would like that. I know I wouldn't."

Bick stood with the butt of the borrowed rifle on the ground, his
left hand around the barrel. "This makes twice tonight that you've
gone down there and made a damn fool out of yourself, and twice
you've come running back like a scared jackrabbit, even after you
heard what Hoffer said. Seems you don't pay any attention to what
either him or me says."

Shorty was thinking sadly that this was what responsibility had
done to Tony Bick. Overnight it had changed him from a reckless fun-
loving young hellion into a martinet, a cold-eyed fanatic.

But Shorty was completely unprepared for what happened. In disbelief he saw the gun leap into Bick's hand and explode. In horror he
felt the heavy slug lift him off his feet and slam him to the ground on
his back. Then everything seemed to fade into a whirling darkness.

Bick holstered his smoking gun and said to the astonished hands,
"If anybody else gets the idea I don't mean what I say, just remember
Shorty."

CHAPTER 13

The black stallion tirelessly circled the inside of the corral, making low noises as though muttering to himself. Now and then he emitted an angry blast that Hayden, watching at the window with an uneasy grin, took to be horse profanity.

For the most part the stallion ignored the bay, but now and then he snorted scornfully when he noticed the red horse standing half asleep in the other corral with his rump to the cold wind, or contentedly searching the ground for some overlooked morsel of grain or wild hay. Now if it had been a mare, the stallion might have considered taking her along when he busted out of here. But a gelding—the stallion gave another scornful snort and continued his restless pacing.

When there was shooting, the stallion became even more excited, racing wildly about, and now and then bunching his muscles to leap over the high poles of the corral. But always he changed his mind at the last moment, as though realizing that even he could not clear such a barrier without a better running start than he could get from in here.

There had been no shooting from the hill now in almost an hour, and the waiting was beginning to get on Hayden's nerves. He paced from window to window to peer out into the night, wondering what Hoffer's men were up to even as he held himself tense in expectation of the next volley of lead that would come screaming through the plank wall.

Mead sat in a dark corner, staring at his wet blankets. At last he asked, "Why didn't we use your blankets?"

"Yours were handy. And you said they were already wet."

"They're not just wet now," Mead said. "They've got dirt and ashes all over them. One has, anyway."

"That reminds me," Hayden said. "Where's the water bucket?"

"I guess it's still down there at the spring."

"Then why don't you trot down there and get it. You may get thirsty before the night is over."

"I should have known better than to say anything," Mead grumbled as he got to his feet. He opened the door, then stopped and looked around at Hayden. "What if that short guy came back? Or some of the others may be down there by now."

"Better take the shotgun," Hayden advised. "Maybe you can hit something with it. And I'll cover you from the window."

"Why don't you go and let me cover you from the window?" Mead asked.

"It wasn't me who left the bucket down there," Hayden told him. "And the way you shoot, you'd be about as likely to hit me as you would Hoffer's men."

Mead got the shotgun and left the shack in silence. It was more and more apparent that he had been better off when he let Hayden do the talking as well as the thinking. And the fewer questions he asked, the fewer Hayden would get a chance to answer. He liked Hayden's answers less all the time.

The wind tore at him with icy fingers as soon as he stepped outside, ripping through his damp clothing and chilling him to the bone. He could not keep from shivering, but he suspected it was as much because of fear as cold. He expected to be shot at from two different directions—the cone-shaped hill poking its rocky finger at the night sky, and the arroyo which began just below the waterhole and made a dark streak through the scattered brush. The arroyo worried him more because it was closer, and he watched it with scared eyes, expecting to see a dozen Hoffer men rise up with blazing guns at any moment. He swept the rim with the shotgun, and once he almost fired at a man-sized bush tossing in the wind.

Out of the corner of his eye he could see the stallion trotting about the corral like a wild black demon, tossing his head. For a moment his glance went to the shed, behind which someone might be waiting, watching him through a crack. But he thought it unlikely that anyone could have reached the shed without being spotted by Hayden's hawk eyes.

Nothing happened. No shots were fired. He filled the bucket and got back to the shack with a feeling of real accomplishment. Not because he had recovered the bucket, but because he was still alive.

Hayden had been watching through the small window, and turned his head to grin at him as he came in.

Mead frowned as he set the bucket on the shelf. "Well, you didn't get me killed this time, Hayden. But keep trying. You may manage it yet."

Hayden's grin faded. "You don't strike me as a man who needs any help. You'll soon get that done all by yourself, the way you're going."

"I knew I should keep my mouth shut," Mead muttered. "But all the same, I think I'll let you go after water the next time."

"I think we'll both go the next time," Hayden said after a moment. Mead glanced at him in wonder.

"I've been thinking," Hayden added, again looking out the window. "I don't do it very often, but sometimes there ain't no way of getting out of it. We've been lucky so far, but that can't last. If they keep shooting holes in that wall, sooner or later one of us is bound to get hit."

He was silent a moment. "That arroyo goes both ways. If they can use it, we can too, and it's our turn to pay them a little visit. It wouldn't be polite not to. We'll wait till just before daylight, when they're all good and sleepy. Then we'll sneak down to that waterhole with the bucket and keg like we're going to get in plenty of water to last through the day. Only we'll have our guns with us, and while we're down there we'll duck out of sigh behind them tall bushes and slip into that arroyo. By the time they figure out what we're up to, maybe we can be in them big rocks at the bottom of that hill."

An hour before dawn, by the clock in Hayden's head, he eased the door open and stood in it for a moment. No shots roared at him from the direction of the arroyo or the shed. Holding his rifle ready in his right hand, he lifted the nearly empty keg with his left and said to Mead, "Bring the bucket and them shells I put on the table. Leave the door open like we were coming right back. On second thought, you better close it real quiet-like, to keep the wind from slamming it and maybe waking them up, if they ain't awake already."

He stepped outside, and no bullets screamed at him from the hill. After a moment Mead came out with the bucket and the shotgun and softly closed the door behind him, turning his head to look toward the silent hill looming up in the darkness. Then they went quietly down toward the waterhole, Mead keeping close behind Hayden.

At the waterhole they bent down behind the clump of tall brush, eased the keg and bucket to the ground, and crawled on to the arroyo, Hayden still in the lead. Even after they were in the arroyo they kept crawling until it became deep enough to hide them from the men on the hill.

At last they stopped to catch their breath and brush the sand from their weapons. The wind blew directly along the arroyo as though using it for a channel. Their faces and hands were numb with cold. Mead fumbled so badly that he dropped the old Starr pistol and had to clean it more carefully than before. Hayden glared at him with silent scorn, cussing himself once more for bringing the greenhorn along. He would have been better off without him.

Then they got to their feet and went on, trudging silently through the deep soft sand and keeping close under the west bank where they could not be seen from the rough slope above. Once Mead stumbled on a rock and fell to his knees with a grunt. Hayden looked around and silently shook his head. But they ran into no serious trouble until they climbed out of the arroyo.

Then, as they rose to their feet, they saw four dark silent figures coming down the steep slope directly toward them. The four men saw them in the same instant and leapt behind rocks as Hayden and Mead also scrambled for the nearest cover, a lone rock ten feet from the arroyo.

"I thought you said they'd all be sound asleep," Mead muttered, kneeling behind the rock as though in prayer.

"I guess they had the same idea," Hayden grunted, peering cautiously over the rock.

A gun roared and the bullet whined angrily off the rock near his head. He ducked and swore softly, then fell silent, listening. There was movement on the dark slope above, the scuff of feet, the mutter of a low voice giving instructions. They were spreading out, seeking vantage points, creeping closer.

He quickly raised his head to look for a target, then ducked again as that same gun sent a burst of thunder and lead his way.

Mead hugged the ground, gripping the shotgun and muttering

prayers or cusses under his breath. Hayden could not tell which. He waited until the gun above clicked on an empty chamber, then he rose with his Winchester ready. Another man, now safely behind a boulder, began blazing away at him. But this one's bullets did not come close enough to make Hayden duck and he fired back, rapidly working the lever on his rifle, and it was the other man who ducked from sight, growling an angry curse.

Hayden swept the slope with a sharp glance and saw another man aiming a rifle over a rock, carefully drawing a bead on him. Hayden threw a slug that way and then jerked his head back down. The other man held his fire. Hayden heard someone reloading.

Hayden glanced at Mead, still hugging the ground. "Let's see your hat."

Mead looked up in wonder. "What for?"

Hayden held out his hand, and after a moment Mead reluctantly took off his hat and gave it to him. Hayden put the hat on the end of his Winchester and stuck it up above the rock. Guns blasted and the hat flew off. Mead cried out angrily as he scrambled to get it.

"Hey! That's a new hat! Why don't you get your own hat shot full of holes!"

"If you get out alive, I figured you might like a souvenir," Hayden told him. "Someday you can show your grandchildren that hat and tell them how you licked the Hoffer gang, with a little help from some old boy named Hayden who hid behind the rock and let you do most of the fighting."

Hayden could see Mead thinking about it as he silently fingered the bullet holes in the crown of his hat.

Hayden took his own hat off and placed it carefully on the ground beside him, for he needed a good hat more than he needed a souvenir. A hat with bullet holes in it would not keep the rain and sleet and snow out, although it might come in handy on hot summer days. He had every intention of getting out of here alive, despite all Mead and the Hoffer bunch could do to prevent it.

He knew it would not be easy, for Mead was more likely to get him killed accidentally than they were on purpose.

"Be careful which way you point that scattergun, Mead. I don't expect you to hit them. Just try not to hit me."

He thumbed several cartridges into the loading gate of his rifle, then leaned the rifle against the rock and checked his Colts, adding a sixth cartridge in the chamber normally left empty. It looked like he would soon need all the firepower he had and then some. By now the rest of Hoffer's men would be working their way down through the rocks. That meant about seven or eight to one, unless you counted Mead. Then it would be eight or nine to one.

A dark shape appeared off to Hayden's left. A gun flashed and roared. He still had a Colt in his hand and he swung it toward the man, thumbing a quick shot. The shotgun blasted right by his ear as the man fell, almost deafening him.

"I got him!" Mead cried excitedly.

Hayden jerked his head around to glare at the greenhorn in amazement and rage. "Got him, hell! You damn near got me, you fool!"

CHAPTER 14

The darkness was already fading. The clock in Hayden's head had been wrong. He should have gone outside to check the sky, a more reliable timepiece. If he had waited a little longer it would not have been necessary to go outside, for he could have seen the sky graying in the east.

They would soon be exposed here. There was only one rock about four feet high and a few stunted shrubs. The next cover was a good twenty feet away, beyond an open stretch.

There was some quiet scurrying around in the rocks above. The word had been passed in whispers and Hoffer's men were using the last darkness to retreat to higher ground, where they could fire down on Hayden and Mead with rifles.

Mead seemed to be smiling to himself in an abstracted way as he fondled the shotgun. In his mind he was no doubt rehearsing the story he would tell his grandchildren—provided he lived to have any.

Hayden rudely interrupted the daydream, prodding him with a boot toe.

The man who lay off to Hayden's left was Hoke Kelsey. The growing light revealed a murderous scowl on his bearded face. His eyes were narrowed to glittering slits. His teeth were clenched against the pain in his side. His left hand was pressed tightly against the wound to check the bleeding. His right hand moved slowly and cautiously over the ground, searching for the gun he had dropped. He was out of rifle shells and had left his Winchester behind, but his .45 was somewhere nearby, if he could just find it. He had dropped it when he fell, so it could not be far from where he lay.

His hand froze when he heard the big man say, "Come alive, Mead. We can't stay here. We'll have to move before it gets any lighter."

"We going back?" Mead asked in a half-hopeful tone.

Hayden seemed offended by the suggestion. "Not on your life. It was too much trouble to get this far, and it would be even more trouble the next time. They'd be laying for us. No, we're going on, Mead. Straight up that hill. And you're going to lead the charge."

"Why me?"

"When you're blazing away with that scattergun," Hayden replied, "I feel a lot safer with you in front of me than behind me."

Hoke Kelsey's right hand resumed the painstaking search for his gun.

"I want you to get set," Hayden said, "and then I want you to come up shooting and head for them rocks as fast as you can go. I'll stay here and cover for you. Then you can cover for me."

Hoke Kelsey's big hand became almost frantic in its search for the elusive weapon.

"You set?" Hayden asked quietly.

"I'm set," Mead said in a doubtful tone.

"Then go," Hayden told him. "It's almost sunup."

Mead came up blasting from the hip with the shotgun and leapt over the rock, when he could have easily stepped around it. Hoke Kelsey, watching through slitted eyes, almost snorted his scorn before he thought. Then Hayden was firing his Winchester rapidly over the rock to keep the Hoffer men ducking while Mead streaked across the open stretch.

The rim of the sun appeared suddenly in the east, bathing the rocky hill in crimson light. Hayden groaned under his breath and Hoke Kelsey smiled.

The Winchester began clicking, and to Kelsey's surprise Hayden did not take time to reload. He suddenly rose and ran toward the rocks, waving the rifle high in the air and yelling, "Hold your fire!"

Tony Bick and the others held their fire, gawking at him in wonder. But Hoke Kelsey pushed himself up to a sitting position and looked frantically about for his gun.

When Hayden was almost to the rocks he grinned and said,

"Thanks!"

High on the hill Tony Bick stamped his foot and screamed, "Sonofabitch! We're all a bunch of damn fools!"

At last Kelsey found his gun, but Hayden had already ducked into the rocks. Kelsey glared at the gun with murderous rage, as though it had deliberately hidden from him until it was too late to be of any use.

But maybe he could still get them, if he took his time and moved with care. Otherwise he knew he was a dead man.

From her window Rose saw Hoffer down at the corral, saddling his horse. Her lips twisted with resentment and scorn as she watched him. She hated the sight of his bullneck and potbelly. Why her mother had ever married him, she could not begin to imagine, and she did not blame her mother in the least for trying to leave him. She only blamed Hoffer for stopping her and causing her death.

Hoffer glanced slyly over his shoulder at the house, then left his horse tied to a post and let down the gate bars. Rose's dark eyes flashed with anger when she saw him drive the other horses out and chase them off. She should have known that was what he would do, she told herself.

Hoffer led his chestnut gelding up to the house and a moment later she heard him come in. He knocked on her door and said, "All right, Rose. You win. I can't let you stay in there and starve. I'm going to town. I've got to see Boyle at the store. But don't you try to go off anywhere while I'm gone."

"How can I?" she retorted. She was so angry she could not speak calmly. "You ran all the horses off and I've got a sprained ankle!"

She thought she heard him chuckle, but was not sure. Then he cleared his throat and said, "I'll see if I can get some medicine for your ankle, and you better stay off it for a few days. That's the main thing. And be sure to eat something. We'll talk when I get back."

"We won't talk when you get back!" she yelled through the locked door. "We have nothing more to say to each other!"

"I'll be back about noon," Hoffer said in a harsher, almost threatening tone. "I want you to do some serious thinking while I'm gone. And when I get back I want you out of that room, and I want to find a hot meal on the table."

"Then you better send the cook up here to fix it for you!" she cried. "I'll never fix you another meal as long as I live!"

"We'll see about that," Hoffer said, and went out slamming the door. A moment later she heard him ride off at a fast trot.

She waited until the sound of his horse faded in the distance, and then she got the door unlocked and open with trembling hands. She rushed to the kitchen and started grabbing anything that looked like food and stuffing it into her mouth. Then she suddenly quit eating and sat down in a chair, holding her stomach.

Later, when she felt like it, she began carrying food to her room and hiding it.

Hoffer's bulldog jaw was set in cold anger as he followed the dusty trail north toward town. It was not enough that he had to put up with stupid, lazy hands and stubborn squatters. His stepdaughter had to defy him as well. But he would show her. He would make her mind or wish she had.

The trail dipped into a ravine that curved around the bottom of an isolated butte with a talus slope at its base. Hoffer abruptly drew rein, shocked to find the tall red-bearded man sitting a horse directly in his path.

"You!" Hoffer cried hoarsely.

"So it appears," the tall man said in an idle tone. There was no particular expression on his sunburnt face, but his blue eyes were incredibly cold. "That fellow who helps out around the general store in town asked me to pass on a message if I saw you," he added. "He said he'd go ahead and bury Whitey Cruger for you."

"Did you kill him?" Hoffer asked. "Or was it Hayden?"

The tall man watched him blankly and made no reply.

"Let's not waste time," Hoffer said harshly. "I know why you're here. But killing me won't do you any good. I can make it worth your while to ride on out of the country and forget you ever saw me."

He reached inside his coat, and without the slightest hesitation the tall man drew his gun and shot him in the center of his broad body.

For a long moment Hoffer sat very still in his saddle, a thick wallet in his hand and a sick look on his face.

"You should have known better than that, Hoffer," the tall man said without mercy or regret. "Remember what happened to that old man down in Texas? He reached for a deed to his land and some wild young men thought he was reaching for a gun."

"How did you know about that?" Hoffer gasped, his face slack and gray.

The tall man shrugged, smoke curling lazily from the muzzle of his gun. "Word gets around. You should know by now that a big man like you can't have any secrets. He's the center of attention. Everything he does or says is news. But nobody pays any attention to a little man like me. I can just ride on out of the country and no one will ever know I was here."

"But you won't, will you?" Hoffer said bitterly.

"Not till I finish what I came back to do."

Hoffer sat staring at him through a haze of pain and hatred. Then an odd look came into the rancher's eyes. "Tell Rose," he whispered, "tell her . . . tell the bitch nothing. She's just like her mother."

Then, staring straight ahead with unseeing eyes, he slipped out of the saddle.

Rose went to the window when she heard the horse coming. Her heart started pounding. It was Hoffer's chestnut and Hoffer was facedown across the saddle. The horse stopped in front of the house. Rose hurried outside and saw that Hoffer's hands and feet had been tied together under the horse's belly. He had been shot through the body. Blood dripped to the ground as she watched. She felt sick again.

The fat, white-haired cook was suddenly at her side, staring in disbelief at the dead rancher.

"Get him down," Rose said. "We'll have to bury him."

"Can't it wait till the hands get back?" the old cook complained.

She glanced off toward the mesa. "There's no telling when they'll get back. They may not get back at all. And I want him buried before I leave."

The cook gaped at her in disbelief. "You going to leave, Miss Rose?"

She looked at Hoffer and tears filled her eyes. "I thought I wanted to leave to get away from him," she said. "But now that he's dead there doesn't seem to be any reason to stay here. I thought I hated him. I thought I wanted him dead, but now ..." Her voice trailed off and she shook her head.

"What about the rest of us, Miss Rose?" the cook whined.

"I guess you'll just have to look for another job," she told him. "Crown is finished."

Tony Bick stood his Winchester against the rock beside him and checked his white-handled Colt. "Where's Kelsey?" he asked the nearest man, who was called Big Nose Sam because he had a huge bulbous nose that did nothing to improve his pockmarked swarthy face.

"I guess Hayden got him," Big Nose said. "Hoke could move mighty quiet for such a big man, but not quiet enough, I guess."

"Yeah, I think Hoke got hisself filled full of lead," another man said, blowing on his cold hands. "I heard Hayden and that greenhorn both blastin' away at him and then I heard him fall. Sounded like a big old oak tree comin' down."

"Sonofabitch," Tony Bick muttered, slipping a sixth cartridge into the cylinder of his gun. "If we don't start being more careful, the bastard will get us all."

"It don't seem rightly possible that he could get us all," Big Nose said, fondling an old Spencer as his beady black eyes scanned the rocks below. "Not just him and that greenhorn."

"That greenhorn will just get in his way," drawled a tall stoop-shouldered man called Slim. "And he can't move without us spottin' him, now that it's gettin' light. I figger we should bag him before long."

As Slim spoke, a bullet whined off the rock near him, knocking dust and fragments into his face. He ducked and swore softly.

"What was you sayin', Slim?" snickered the youngest hand, a tow-headed youth still in his teens, but no stranger to trouble and evil deeds.

Big Nose Sam hoisted his old Spencer and fired a couple of rounds at Hayden's smoke.

"Get him?" Slim asked, keeping low.

"Never even saw him," Big Nose said.

"He ain't got your hawk eye, Slim," said the young hand named Max.

"Stop wasting your bullets," Tony Bick said. "We've wasted too many already. And stop talking. By now he knows where we all are."

"We know where he is too," Big Nose said.

"Yeah, but we don't know he'll stay there," Tony Bick said.

Big Nose's ugly face got red. "Seems like it was your idea for us to pull back."

"That was when he was down there near the arroyo," Bick said. "What I had in mind was for us to get the top of that rock in our sights and all fire at the same time when he raised his head. But we all stood here like a bunch of fools and let him get in them big rocks. Now our best bet is to spread out and close in on him and that greenhorn, before they sneak up on us. But watch where you shoot, and make your shots count."

CHAPTER 15

Cradling the shotgun in his arms, Mead rubbed his hands to warm them and glanced over his shoulder at the sun, still only a ball of cold fire above the eastern horizon. "I'll sure be glad when it warms up a little," he said.

Hayden thumbed a cartridge into the loading gate of his rifle. "Don't hold your breath. The wind will get started blowing any minute now and it will seem colder than ever."

"It's blowing a little now. I don't think it ever stops blowing in this country, does it?"

"Frank Martin said it stopped for a while the first summer he was here. I was gone off someplace. Idaho, I think."

"You must stay gone a big part of the time," Mead said.

Hayden's face was drawn and bleak. "Too much, I guess. If I'd been here when Frank needed me, he might still be alive."

Mead's hands reluctantly closed around the cold steel and wood of the shotgun. "If he was as good with a pistol as you say, what did he need with a shotgun?"

"He hardly ever used it. He only kept it to discourage trouble-makers and for night fighting when he couldn't see well enough to use a pistol. When we were in Texas we used to have a lot of trouble with Comanches trying to steal our horses at night. They got so they dreaded that shotgun and didn't come around very often."

"You and him must have been pretty close," Mead said.

"Not as close as we should have been," Hayden replied. "But I guess we were about as close as me or him could get to anyone."

"Neither of you ever married?"

"No. Never ran into the right girl, I guess."

"What about Rose Hoffer. You think she might be the right girl?"

Hayden smiled bleakly. "I don't think it matters much now. She'll hate my guts before this is over, if she don't already."

Rose Hoffer stood beside the chestnut gelding, looking off toward the mesa with bitter eyes. She had removed Hoffer's bloodstained saddle and put her own saddle in its place. She had put on her riding clothes and a warm coat, and there was a bundle of extra clothes tied on behind the saddle, the same bundle she had planned to take with her when she left with Francisco. Now she would go alone, but not penniless. Her right hand rested on the bulging saddlebags she had found in her father's safe.

She had also found a gun in the safe, a short-barreled double-action Webley .44, the kind called a Bulldog. Most Webleys were made in England, but this was an American Webley, made in New York City. It said so on the barrel. The gun was now in her coat pocket, and loaded. She knew how to use it. Hoffer had taught her, before locking the gun in the safe.

The fat cook stood nearby, his eyes damp, glancing at the blisters on his pudgy hands. The blisters seemed to bother him more than Hoffer's death, now that the shock had worn off. "We should of sent word to Boyle," he complained. "He takes care of the undertaking around here. Got a man who's used to that sort of thing."

Rose was still looking toward the mesa and did not seem to hear him. But after a moment she said, "If he's not, I imagine he will be before this is over."

She handed the cook some money and added, "This is for you. If any of the men come back complaining about their wages, tell them they can steal any cows they can find. I'm sure that's what they'll do anyway."

"Ain't no cows much left, Miss Rose," the cook said. "Mr. Hoffer sold most of them a while back. He was planning to get a big herd cheap in Mexico."

"Well, I don't guess he'll be cheating the Mexicans out of any more cattle," Rose said. "Or anything else." Including me, she thought. But the bitterness she had felt toward Hoffer was gone. She would not have believed it was possible two days ago, but she missed him more than she missed Francisco, regretted his death more than Francisco's.

She stepped carefully into the saddle, favoring her sore ankle, said a rather curt goodbye to the old cook and rode off, heading east toward the mesa.

Helen Mead kept going to the window to look out, hoping to see her husband and Hayden ride up, but afraid she would see Hoffer's men instead. She would not put it past that bunch to bring their bodies and dump them in the yard, gloating over their bloody victory and abusing her. She was worried sick.

She did not know what she would do if Carl was killed. Going on to California would not mean much without him. If Hayden was still alive and decided to stay in this country, she might stay also. One day perhaps. . . she blushed, shocked at her thoughts. She hoped both of them would return alive and unhurt.

She cooked breakfast for them but they did not appear. She kept the fire going and the coffee hot in case they showed up. She knew that was the first thing they would want on a cold morning, a cup of strong black coffee. She had worked in a restaurant long enough to know that.

She went to the window again—and gasped in surprise, her heart beating faster. She had heard no one ride up, but there was a tall man with a red beard sitting out there on a lean horse, his back to the sun, watching the house with very cold eyes.

She shivered, wondering what she should do. She had no gun. Hayden had offered to leave her one, but she had said she would not know how to use it and would probably be safer without it. Now she was not so sure.

She waited, hoping the tall man would ride on. But he remained there on his white-sprinkled red horse, staring at the house. Once he seemed to look directly at her.

At last she opened the door, watching him carefully, but did not speak.

He slowly touched the brim of his old hat. There was a hole in the crown of the hat, and around the hole a stain that she thought was a bloodstain that had been partly removed and then covered with dust to disguise it. He looked tired and gaunt, but ready to strike with sudden deadliness if he was threatened from any quarter. The polished walnut stock of a gun showed below his dirty, ragged coat.

"Ma'am," he said. "I'd be obliged to water my horse. May be a while before I get a chance again."

"Help yourself." She nodded toward the plank trough that was kept full by a rusty pipe suspended above it. The pipe came from a slow but never-failing trickle of water from the rocky mesa wall behind the house.

The tall man silently dismounted and filled his canteen at the trickle from the pipe while the horse drank. She noticed that the man did not drink himself. He hung the canteen back on the saddle horn and then glanced at her. There was no hint of a smile on his face when he spoke, no lessening of the quiet gravity. "That coffee sure smells good, ma'am. I've got a tin cup in my saddlebag. I'd be obliged if you'd bring me a cup."

She hesitated, studying him. There was something in his cold empty eyes that frightened her, and yet somehow she felt sure that he meant her no harm. "All right," she said.

He got the cup from his saddlebag and brought it to her and waited outside until she came back. She handed him the cup of smoking black coffee, and a brown paper bag. "Some bacon and biscuits, in case you're hungry," she said.

"Obliged." He glanced at her and frowned slightly. "How much do I owe you?"

"That's all right," she said, knowing it was the custom of the country to feed strangers without asking for pay. Many people violated the custom but she thought it best not to. She studied him thoughtfully while he sipped the coffee. She noticed that his chestnut hair and beard had been trimmed recently, but it did not appear to be a very professional job. "I don't usually behave this way," she added, "but there's been some trouble and I'm a little uneasy."

"I understand, ma'am," he said, moving toward his horse. He put the sack in his saddlebag, then stood by the horse and finished drinking his coffee in silence, his eyes studying the mesa rim and the trail to town. Then he put the cup back in the saddlebag and stepped easily into the saddle, his slow deliberate movements reminding her of Hayden.

"I think I know who you are," Helen said, watching him in wonder and fascination and a little fear.

The coldness of his eyes did not encourage further talk. He touched his hat again and said, "I'm obliged to you, ma'am."

Helen Mead stood at the door, shivering in the cold as she watched him ride off. He took the trail toward town, but she felt certain that when he was out of sight he would climb the mesa wall.

There had been no shooting now for some time, and Hoffer's men were keeping out of sight. But Hayden could sense movement in the rocks, even though he could not quite hear it. They were closing in.

He heard his stomach growl. "A big pot of hot coffee would sure go good about now," he muttered. "It makes me wish we'd stayed in the shack."

"It makes me wish I'd stayed home," Mead said. "I could sit around and drink coffee all day."

Hayden glanced at him out of one cold eye. "I figured you'd rather go into town and sit around that restaurant all day."

"That girl don't mean anything to me, if that's what you're thinking," Mead said. "It's just that I've got in the habit of sitting around restaurants and drinking coffee."

"And talking to the waitress who pours it?"

Mead nodded. "That too, I guess."

"Well, we better shut up," Hayden grunted, "and keep our eyes peeled. I think I heard someone moving around up there a minute ago."

After a moment Mead said in a low tone, "Hayden."

Hayden glanced at him. Mead had his head turned the other way. "I thought I just told you to shut up."

"I just saw a bush move up there about twenty feet," Mead whispered, sounding a little scared.

Hayden was not sure which bush he meant, as there were gray shrubs and a few stunted green cedars scattered over the rocky slope. "You sure it wasn't caused by the wind?"

"I don't think so. The wind ain't blowing that hard. I think there's somebody behind it, moving the branches to look through. There's a rock below the bush."

"The next time you see it move," Hayden told him, "blast it with that scattergun."

"It just moved again," Mead said.

"Then blast it."

There was a little click as Mead cocked the hammer. Then he quickly raised the shotgun and fired. There was a startled yelp from behind the cedar, and then the sound of a man diving to the ground and scrambling away on all fours.

Hayden grinned. "He'll be picking out buckshot for a while. Looks like bringing you along wasn't such a bad idea after all."

"Don't give yourself too much credit," Mead said as he broke the shotgun open and removed the empty shell. "It wasn't your idea."

"I may live to regret it yet," Hayden replied, scanning the slope in the opposite direction.

The shot came without warning, from somewhere above him. The bullet whistled past his ear and he jerked his head down too quickly to see the puff of smoke from the muzzle.

"You ain't scared of bullets, are you, Hayden?" Mead asked in a dry tone.

"It takes a fool not to be scared of bullets," Hayden snarled.

"It's only when I hear them whine off a rock that they scare me," Mead said. "That's when I start ducking."

"The ones you hear whine off a rock have already done what damage they're going to do," Hayden told him.

"I notice you usually duck pretty fast."

"I guess they scare me too," Hayden admitted. "But you won't hear the one that kills you."

"That's a cheering thought."

"Shut up. I heard something."

What he had heard was a small rock rolling down the slope not far away. A rock dislodged by a careless step. That was his guess, anyway.

"Stay here and keep your eyes peeled," he whispered.

He laid the rifle gently on the ground, knowing it would impede his progress, and drew the Colt from the cross-draw holster on the left and began wriggling his way through the rocks toward the sound he had heard.

He had not gone three feet when the shotgun blasted behind him. He glanced quickly over his shoulder. "See somebody?"

"No, but I saw another bush move," Mead said.

Hayden scowled. "Don't let it go to your head just because you were right once. Every bush on this hill is moving. In case you ain't noticed, the wind just started blowing."

Mead was silent, his face turning red.

Hayden glared at him a moment and then worked his way carefully on around the rocky slope. When he had gone ten feet he paused to listen, then went on.

A small rock hit the ground nearby, and he realized he had been tricked. Somebody was tossing the rocks from somewhere else to draw his attention this way, when he needed to be watching in another direction. The oldest trick in the book and I fell for it, he thought.

He raised his head cautiously and peered in the direction from which he believed the rock had come, but saw only the gray rocks, and the gray brush stirring in the cold wind, and the rocky spire at the top of the hill pointing at the hazy blue sky like a church steeple. The mocking irony was lost on Hayden. He had other things on his mind—the harsh realization that it was kill or be killed. To hesitate or show mercy would be to die at the hands of men who would sneer at his stupidity.

He turned himself carefully around and faced back the way he had come, but remained where he was, watching. Frequently he turned his head to look in every direction. All morning he'd had the itchy feeling that someone was trying to creep up on him from behind. But under the circumstances that was to be expected.

Another small rock or gravel hit the ground off to his right. Instinctively he turned his head and his gun in that direction, even though he had warned himself not to. He made an even worse mistake. He cocked the hammer of his gun. The small double click sounded startlingly loud in the silence. He cussed himself under his breath for behaving like a greenhorn. Even Mead could have done no worse, not without working at it.

A moment later he changed his mind.

The shotgun roared, then roared again. He saw Mead up on his feet gawking upslope as he fumbled for shells.

"Get down, you fool!" Hayden yelled.

Mead glanced toward him, then quickly ducked behind the rock. A fraction of a second later guns blasted at him from at least three different directions.

Mead quickly raised back up and again emptied both barrels of the shotgun.

Hayden shook his head and muttered to himself, "That fool will get us both killed yet."

For now all of Hoffer's men knew where he, Hayden, was, if there had been any doubt in their minds before.

No point in hanging around here now and waiting to get picked off by a sneaky marksman. Better go back and caution Mead against further blunders. He crawled back to where the greenhorn was and fixed him in a chilly gaze.

"I see you aim to get yourself killed regardless," he said. "What were you doing up there in plain sight gawking like a greenhorn?"

"I was trying to see if I got that man I shot at."

"And while you were trying to see if you got him, any of the others might have got you."

"I didn't think," Mead admitted.

"*Did* you get him?" Hayden asked.

"I don't think so."

"How far away was he?"

"About fifteen feet."

Hayden stared at him in amazement. "How did you manage to miss a man fifteen feet away with a shotgun?"

Mead lifted one hand from the shotgun to rub his right eye. "Well, he dived behind a rock as soon as he saw me and I didn't get a good shot at him."

"I knew you'd have some excuse," Hayden grunted. Then he asked, "Do you think you can stay out of trouble if I leave you here by yourself for a while?"

Mead glanced uneasily at him. "Where are you going?"

"Not far. They know where we are. I want to get off to one side a piece and keep an eye peeled."

"And leave me here like a sitting duck."

Hayden nodded. "That's about the size of it. There's no point in you getting us both killed."

"Ain't you afraid I'll miss them and hit you?" Mead asked.

"Not a chance. I aim to keep plenty of cover between me and you."

"I figured that was why you wanted to get away from me," Mead said.

"I didn't realize it was so plain even a greenhorn could see it," Hayden grunted, and moved off through the rocks like a three-legged snail, taking his rifle along this time.

Mead watched him go in silence. One moment he thought he liked Hayden. The next he was sure he hated him. But one thing was certain. He felt a lot safer when the big man was close by. Not more comfortable, just safer.

Mead leaned the shotgun against the rock and drew the Starr pistol from its holster. He liked the way the heavy old revolver felt in his hand. Too bad he could not hit anything with it.

He had his head bent looking at the gun when he heard feet moving quietly off to his left. He had come from a town where the sound of footsteps was no cause for alarm and it was a moment before the alarm bell started ringing in his head. That moment almost cost him his life.

He turned his head and saw a grinning, evil-looking boy taking deliberate aim at him with a huge pistol.

With a hoarse cry Mead flung himself to the rocky ground on his belly just as the boy fired. He heard the buzz of the bullet a foot above his head and saw the gun jump in the boy's hand. Then he saw the boy leap almost casually behind a rock as Mead jerked up the old Starr and began frantically pulling the trigger. He kept pulling the trigger even after he could no longer see the boy. He kept pulling it until the gun began clicking. Then he dropped the pistol and grabbed the shotgun. With a trembling hand he cocked both hammers and waited for another glimpse of that grinning, evil young face. He knew the boy was over there behind the rocks, not much over ten feet away, waiting for a chance to kill him.

There was a snicker from behind the rocks. Then the boy said in a taunting voice, "Hey, greenhorn. I'm going to kill you, did you know that, greenhorn?"

Mead knew the boy would kill him if he got a chance.

Mead heard a small sound on the slope above him. He listened, and for a moment heard only the pounding of his own heart and the rustling of the wind in the brush. Then he heard the crunch of gravel under a heavy boot. Someone was moving down the slope toward him.

The boy's grinning face suddenly appeared above the rock, then disappeared an instant before the shotgun roared.

Mead realized what the boy's game was. He knew Mead's pistol was empty, and now he was trying to make him empty the shotgun. Then the grinning boy would kill him.

"Hayden!" Mead yelled. "I only got one shell in the shotgun, no chance to reload, and there's men all around me!"

There was no answer from Hayden.

The boy snickered again. "It won't be long now, greenhorn. If you know any prayers, you better say them."

The boy suddenly rose up with the gun in his hand. Mead fired instantly, before the boy had time to duck, but he forgot to take aim before he pulled the trigger. The load of buckshot went harmlessly over the boy's head.

Then Mead turned and ran the way Hayden had gone, yelling the big man's name.

"Hayden!"

Chapter 16

Hayden appeared beside a huge boulder with his Winchester half raised. He seemed to be glaring at Mead and past him at the same time. "Mead! Get down, you fool!"

Mead did not get down. He was too scared. He kept running toward Hayden as fast as he could pump his legs, trying to outrun the bullets Hoffer's men were shooting at him.

Hayden swore softly and began firing to give him cover, working the lever rapidly and shifting the muzzle from target to target, firing at puffs of smoke and almost anything else he saw. There was no time to take aim or make sure of his target. Mead kept running toward him and yelling, and showed every intention of going on by at the same wild gallop, but Hayden stuck out a boot and sent him sprawling, then went on firing as he backed into the rocks. When the Winchester was empty he shifted it to his left hand and emptied one of his Colts.

Mead was trying to rise again.

"Stay down, you fool!"

Hayden roughly grabbed the greenhorn by the collar of his coat and dragged him behind a rock, then shoved him back down hard.

"Stay there and load that scattergun!" Hayden snarled. "Always keep one gun loaded!"

"What if you've only got one?" Mead managed to say as he fumbled for shells with a cold trembling hand.

"Then keep it loaded!"

Mead blinked but said nothing. By then he had learned that it was best to keep his mouth shut around Hayden. It was just that he forgot at times.

Hayden was staring at his holster. "Where's your handgun?"

Mead's hand went to his holster. It was empty. He looked back the way he had come. "I think I dropped it back there. It was empty, though."

Hayden's dark brows knitted in savage scorn. "Oh, it was empty, so you just left it lay!"

"I mean—I forgot it," Mead stammered.

"Then it looks like you'll just have to trot back out there and get it," Hayden told him. "It might help you to remember the next time."

Mead's eyes widened in alarm. "That crazy boy will kill me! And he's probably got the gun by now."

"It would serve you right," Hayden said. "But you'd probably come back without the shotgun this time, and you need it more." He was reaching for cartridges as he spoke. "Better give me them shells before you lose them too. I'm about out, thanks to your little escapade."

Mead looked at him in wonder. "What shells?"

"What do you mean, what shells? The ones I told you to bring. Don't tell me you came off and forgot them."

Mead shook his head. "I don't know anything about any shells, except for about half a box of shotgun shells you left on the table."

"I put a box of .44s beside the shotgun shells," Hayden said, his own eyes widening in alarm now. "You mean you didn't bring them?"

"You should have told me," Mead said. "All I saw was that box of shotgun shells. It was too dark in there to see anything."

Hayden's big hand moved carefully around the back part of his shell belt where he could not see. Almost all the loops were empty. The alarm in his eyes was giving way to hopeless resignation. Suddenly he sat down on a rock with a weary sigh. "That's great," he said. "Just great."

"It serves you right for trying to use me for a pack animal," Mead said, embarrassed and resentful.

"It's all you're fit for," Hayden replied. Then he asked, "How many shotgun shells have you got left?"

Mead felt in his pockets. "Just two."

"Two!" Hayden echoed.

Mead flushed. "And I didn't reload it yet. I took them shells out of the box and put them in my pockets so they'd be easier to carry, but some of them must have dropped out while we were crawling down that arroyo."

"That's great," Hayden said again. "Now we've got about half a dozen shells between us that we can use."

"Well," Mead said, "I guess we'll just have to make every shot count. There can't be more than about six of Hoffer's men left."

Somehow he knew at once that he should not have said that. He knew it even before Hayden answered with biting sarcasm. "Oh, I see. That's all we've got to do. After wasting lead like it was the Fourth of July, now all of a sudden we're going to start making every shot count."

Mead bent his head in shame—and noticed the shells in his cartridge belt. His eyes brightened. "Won't my shells fit your guns? They're .44s."

"Guess I forgot to mention it," Hayden said in the same savage tone, "but there are about six different sizes of .44 shells. A few years back Colt brought out a handgun that uses the same shells as the '73 Winchester. That's why I bought the ones I'm wearing. But your shells are different. So it looks like I may still have to send you back after that old Starr pistol. It looks like we're going to need it."

Mead sat on the ground in silence for a long moment. Then he thoughtfully put the last two shells into the shotgun and got to his feet. "Well, if I don't make it back—"

"Sit back down," Hayden snarled. "I'll tell you when to go."

Mead readily obeyed, with no back talk.

He watched Hayden. The big man held three cartridges in his hand, studying them with frowning concentration. After a moment he thumbed them into his Winchester. Then he punched the empty shells from the Colt and put it back in the holster, empty. But his other Colt was still fully loaded.

"What are our chances now?" Mead asked, dreading the answer.

"Don't ask," Hayden grunted, watching for Hoffer's men. After a moment he added bitterly, "By myself I might have had a slim chance. But I should have known I wouldn't have any chance at all if I brought a greenhorn like you along."

Mead studied the ground in silence.

Hayden moved away from him and took up a position behind a chest-high rock, preferring his own company.

When he looked around, Mead was gone.

Mead worked his way carefully through the rocks, circling toward the place where he had been before, shotgun at the ready. Twice he stopped to listen, but heard nothing, saw nothing. If Hoffer's men were moving around they were being mighty quiet about it. Perhaps they were still where they had been when they were doing all that shooting, waiting for another shot at Hayden or Mead. He hoped so. He did not want to blunder into anyone unexpectedly.

His face heated when he thought of how he had panicked before. He did not know what had come over him. He had been in more danger turning his back and running than if he had stayed where he was and quickly reloaded the shotgun. Hoffer's men would have almost certainly killed him if Hayden had not spoiled their aim with a burst of rifle and pistol fire.

Mead was scared now, and his palms were damp with sweat despite the cold. But he was determined not to panic this time.

When he believed he was getting close, he got down on his hands and knees and crawled, being careful not to bump the shotgun on the rocky ground. There was a clump of gray brush just ahead that looked familiar. When he got to it he peered through the branches and saw the evil-looking boy squatting behind a rock, cupping a cigarette in his hand and fanning the smoke so it would scatter as it rose.

Mead's heart was pounding. His thumb was slippery. But he managed to cock the hammer of the shotgun, and then he stood up so he could fire over the brush. The towheaded boy dropped his cigarette and spun around, his eyes widening in disbelief when he saw Mead and the twin muzzles of the shotgun gaping at him. The boy was frantically bringing up his revolver when the load of buckshot blasted him back about eight feet.

Mead dived straight into the brush, tore his way out of it like a frantic swimmer and crawled rapidly to the spot where he had dropped his pistol.

The pistol was gone.

Thinking the boy might have taken it, Mead crawled to where he lay. But he could not find the Starr. One of the other men must have got the gun, and might still be close by. Mead quickly unbuckled the dead boy's cartridge belt and tugged it free even though most of the loops were empty. He grabbed the big pistol the boy had dropped, and began working his way back through the rocks the way he had come.

He got back to where Hayden was with no further trouble, and proudly displayed the cartridge belt and revolver. "I couldn't find the Starr, but I got these."

As he might have expected, Hayden was merely annoyed because he had taken a foolish chance and had so little to show for it. "How many cartridges are there?" the big man asked.

Mead's elation began to evaporate as he counted the cartridges. "Four in the belt. Five in the gun. Nine in all. But they're big ones, .45 caliber."

"We need .44s," Hayden told him. "And we need a lot more than nine."

Mead threw the belt down in disgust. It seemed that there was just no way to please Hayden. He had risked his life and this was the thanks he got.

Yet he could understand Hayden's frame of mind. They stood almost no chance of getting out of here alive, and it was largely Mead's fault. Hoffer's men would kill them, as they had killed Frank Martin, and there would be no one to avenge their death. Their murderers would never be punished.

A rider on a roan horse leisurely approached the old shack, keeping it between him and the rocky hill where the shots were being fired. He left his horse out of sight on the north side of the shack and stood at the corner of the shack for several minutes, looking toward the corral with interest. The black stallion spotted him at once, pricked his ears and stared at him as at an irreconcilable foe. The bay's eyes were friendly and for a brief moment a similar expression was reflected in the tall man's eyes.

Then his eyes turned cold again as he glanced toward the rocky hill. The firing had stopped. He walked quietly to the door of the shack and stepped inside, his hand going to the butt of his holstered gun. His sharp blue eyes saw all there was to see in a quick glance— the window with the glass knocked out, the blankets and saddlebags on the floor, the box of cartridges on the table, the black suit hanging on the wall.

The tall man glanced down at the dirty, ragged clothes he wore. After a moment he took them off and put on the black suit. It fitted him perfectly.

He took off his old hat, looked at it ruefully and put it back on. He buckled his gun belt back on, then glanced thoughtfully at the box of cartridges on the plank table. He slipped the box into his coat pocket, even though the cartridges would not fit his gun. They were .44 Winchester cartridges. His gun used .44 Smith & Wesson Russian cartridges, although it was not a Russian model.

He stood at the broken window for a time looking thoughtfully at the grave near the shack. Then he stepped outside and glanced up toward the rocky hill. The shooting had started again.

It occurred to Hayden that he almost always regretted it when he let someone talk him into doing something that he believed to be a mistake. He had believed it would be a mistake to bring a greenhorn along—and now, as usual, he was regretting the mistake, and angry with himself for making it.

One moment Mead seemed too scared to do anything right, even if he had known how. The next he took reckless chances that were sure to get him killed before long.

But Helen Mead would not blame her husband if he got himself killed, or herself for asking Hayden to take him along. She would blame Hayden. There was no doubt whatever in Hayden's mind about that. She might never admit it, even to herself, but deep down she would always blame Hayden for not bringing her Carl back to her safe and sound.

"Mead," he said without turning his head, "I want you to get behind me, keep down, keep that scattergun handy and don't let nobody sneak up on my blind side. And don't waste that last shell. If you're not sure of a hit, don't shoot. Just warn me.

"Better let me have that gun you picked up," he added. "There's no way you're going to hit anything with it. You'd just waste the shells."

"All right," Mead said. "But if we get out of this, I want to keep that gun for a souvenir."

"If we get out of this," Hayden replied as he checked the long-barreled .45, "you're welcome to it." He added in a reluctant tone, "I guess you earned it."

He did not turn his head, so he did not see Mead smile.

Big Nose Sam heard quiet footsteps and glanced over his shoulder. It was Tony Bick. Big Nose lowered his gun.

"He get that fool kid?" Bick asked.

Big Nose slowly nodded. "It was that greenhorn. Blasted him with that scattergun. Stayed down and got away before I could get a shot at him. He's learnin'."

"He better learn fast," Tony Bick said, his eyes cold. Then he asked, "Where are the others?"

Big Nose nodded toward the jumble of huge boulders where Hayden and Mead were. "Trying to close in on them. I look for them to get their tails shot off. Slim might not. He's mighty careful with his hide, and sneaky as a old coyote."

Tony Bick was silent. He did not care how many were killed, so long as he was not one of the dead. He hoped he would be the one to kill Hayden, but it did not really matter, so long as Hayden died.

Bick checked his white-handled Colt. Like most of the others, he was out of rifle shells. But at any range up to fifty yards he preferred to use a pistol. "Let's get this over with," he said. "I want to get back in time for chuck."

Big Nose gave him a worried look, remembering what had happened the last time Bick had said that.

Chapter 17

Mead sat on the ground behind Hayden, who stood behind a rock facing the other way. There were big rocks everywhere, and they worried Mead. Hoffer's men could get very close to them without being seen. They might even now be very close.

Mead removed his right hand from the shotgun and wiped his palm on the leg of his trousers. It was so cold it was hard to keep his teeth from chattering, especially when the wind was blowing, and yet there was always sweat on his palms.

Something moved at the corner of his vision. His eyes darted in that direction. He believed something had moved in a shadowy gap between two boulders about thirty feet away, but there was nothing there now.

"Hayden," he said softly, his eyes still glued to the spot, "I think I saw something move in the rocks behind us."

Hayden glanced around. "Where?"

"See that tall rock? Between it and the rock next to it."

"You sure it wasn't the wind moving that bush?"

"I don't think so."

"Keep your eyes peeled," Hayden said, turning his attention back to the slop above. "I imagine they'll be closing in on us from all sides."

A moment later he grunted in surprise and raised the Winchester, but held his fire. "I just saw a hat. But it may be the old hat trick."

"Like when you used my hat?"

"Uh-huh."

Mead took off his hat and looked at the holes in the crown. There were four holes, but he thought that only two bullets had made them. That would be something to show, he thought. Proof that ...

He glanced up, and his mouth sprang open in alarm. There was a man standing beside the tall rock, aiming a rifle at Hayden's broad back. He knew that if he did not spoil the man's aim in time, Hayden would be dead.

So he raised the shotgun and fired at once. The buckshot blasted the rock above the man and to the right, but Mead saw him flinch an instant before the rifle roared, and Mead would always believe that was what saved Hayden's life. For the rifle slug whined harmlessly off the rock a few inches from Hayden's left shoulder, and then the man leaped back out of sight.

"Get him?" Hayden asked as he spun around with the Winchester up, watching for a target.

"No," Mead said.

Hayden shot him a murderous look. "That was your last shell. I told you not to waste it."

Mead was forming an angry reply when a gun roared from the slope above. Hayden whirled back to return the fire, and at that moment the man reappeared beside the tall rock. The man was very tall himself, and thin as a rake. There was an almost friendly look around the eyes that squinted down the rifle barrel toward Mead and Hayden. But there was nothing friendly about the rifle itself.

"Hayden!"

Hayden turned and fired in a split second and Mead saw the bullet knock dust from the rock near the man's head, driving him back to cover. Hayden was already turning back the other way as he jerked the heavy .45 from his waistband and dropped it on the ground beside Mead. A moment later the shell belt, containing four cartridges, hit the ground beside the gun.

"Maybe you can at least scare him," Hayden snarled. "When them shells are gone I guess you'll have to start throwing rocks. I guess we both will. I just wasted two more myself."

Which meant he only had one left in the Winchester, Mead thought. And five or six in the Colt on his right hip. The other Colt was empty. Make every shot count, Mead had said. Even Hayden could not do that. Not in this kind of fighting.

Over the sights of his rifle Hayden watched the spot where he had seen the hat and later the puff of smoke. The sly cruel face of a man in his late twenties suddenly appeared, then ducked from sight again before Hayden could take up the slack on the trigger.

"Hayden!"

Hayden jerked himself around, and knew the instant he did so that it was too late.

The tall skinny man now squatted on top of the tall rock, his head bent, peering through the sights of his rifle at Hayden. He ignored Mead, who had the big .45 up in both hands and ran toward him firing wildly. He kept his undivided attention on Hayden, determined to make this shot count and not be distracted by a harmless greenhorn. In another instant, Hayden knew he would be dead, and he knew there was nothing he could do to stop it. There was no way he could dodge that bullet in time, or get off a shot of his own.

Two shots crowded together in the same explosion. The man on the rock flinched as the bullets hit him. And then he tumbled to the ground below, dropping his rifle as he fell.

"I got him!" Mead cried, staring toward the rock in surprise.

"Got him, hell," Hayden grunted. "You didn't come anywhere near him."

Mead turned around, the excitement in his eyes mingling now with a look of wonder. "I didn't hear you shoot."

"It wasn't me," Hayden said. "Somebody got him with a handgun, but it wasn't you."

"Then who was it?"

There was an odd, almost haunted look in Hayden's eyes as he looked toward the rocks. "I think Frank Martin just returned from the dead. Nobody else can shoot like that."

"What about Hickok? I heard he was pretty good."

"Hickok's dead."

"So is Frank Martin."

"Dead or not," Hayden said, "I've got a feeling that was him."

Mead shivered in the cold wind, and glanced about with uneasy eyes. "If he's a ghost," he said in a low tone, "he may kill us all."

"You, maybe," Hayden said. "I don't think he'd bother me."

"I don't believe in ghosts anyway," Mead said. He kept glancing worriedly about, but he told himself he was watching for Hoffer's men.

There was a cold gleam of amusement in Hayden's pale eyes. A moment later the amusement was replaced by an angry scowl when the bullet tore his black hat off. He had never owned another hat that he liked as well as he did that one. He swung himself around to look for the sneaky marksman on the slope above him. But the man had ducked from sight again.

"You better reload that gun," he said over his shoulder. "You wasted three more bullets, by my count."

"I was trying to save your life!" Mead exclaimed.

"Well, it looks like it took a better man to get the job done," Hayden replied.

A man with dirty brown hair and a small brown mustache moved silently through the rocks behind Hayden and Mead. He stopped in his tracks when he saw the still body of Slim sprawled on the ground by the tall rock. From where he stood he could not see Hayden or Mead, but he knew they were close by. He crept up to the dead man, got his wallet and tobacco, then picked up the rifle, holstering his own revolver.

He stepped over the body and peered around the corner of the rock. He saw Hayden standing about thirty feet away, facing in the other direction, and the greenhorn Mead sitting on a rock nearby, trying to reload a pistol, his attention on what he was doing.

The man with the brown mustache smiled to himself as he raised the rifle.

Hayden had one cartridge left in his Winchester. He was determined to make it count. He knew he was taking a chance, standing there with his back exposed, as well as his head and shoulders above the rock. Yet he stood there motionless, peering through the sights of his rifle.

The sly hard face appeared, started to duck again. Hayden's finger added the final bit of pressure on the trigger. The rifle roared and kicked his shoulder like a wild mustang. A small hole appeared between the surprised eyes of the Hoffer man as his head jerked from sight.

A gun roared behind Hayden, from the direction of the tall rock. He spun around, dropping the empty rifle and drawing his Colt.

But he held his fire, for the man beside the tall rock was already falling, pitching forward to the ground on his face.

A moment later Frank Martin stepped into the open, casually thumbing a cartridge into his gun as he approached. "Morning, Buck," he said as thought nothing of interest had happened since the last time they had seen each other.

Hayden remained silent and watched him carefully, wondering if he was looking at a ghost. But if Frank was a ghost, he had stopped at the shack and put on his black suit.

Mead was darting silent questions at Hayden and uneasy glances at Martin, as if trying to decide whether to shoot or hold his fire. He decided to wait and see what Hayden did.

Martin glanced at Mead through cold eyes. "I see you brung a greenhorn along."

Mead's mouth fell open. He found his voice and asked, half curiously, half resentfully, "What makes you think I'm a greenhorn? You never saw me before—"

"Before Hoffer's men killed me?" Martin asked. "No, it wasn't necessary. I knew there was a greenhorn around here before I ever saw you. Only a greenhorn strews his ammunition like he was leaving a trail for somebody to follow." He took a handful of shells from his pocket and handed them to Mead, then reached into the pocket again and handed Hayden the box of cartridges. "I figgered you might be needing these along about now."

Hayden grinned. "I sure do. Two of my guns are empty and nothing to reload with."

"I won't ask why you came off without them," Martin said, giving Mead another cool glance. "I've got some notions of my own about that." Then he shifted his blue eyes back to Hayden. "I see you caught that black stallion."

Hayden shook his head. "I got him from Hoffer. He broke into Hoffer's corral trying to steal some of his mares, and they grabbed him."

"Well, I figgered all along Hoffer was the type to grab anything he could get his hands on," Martin said. "But don't that beat all? We've been trying to catch that stallion for nigh onto three years, and he goes down there and tears his way into Hoffer's corral. I bet that big stud knew I'd get him sooner or later and did it just to spite me."

"Could be." Hayden looked Martin over again. "I see you put on your black suit."

"Well, I figgered them boys might do a better job of killing me the next time, and I wanted to be ready, just in case."

"What happened, anyway?" Hayden asked.

Martin took off his disreputable looking hat and frowned at it. "Dang wind blew my old hat right down in my face, and before I could get it pushed back up that Tony Bick snuck out a gun and shot me. Bullet just bounced off the side of my head, though. Remember how you always said I had such a hard head? Looks like you were right. It knocked me out for a while, but I've got worse bumps going through low doors. When I woke up they were gone and it was pouring rain. They must have thought I was dead and I decided to let them go on thinking that for a while. I dug me a nice deep grave while that ground was soft and wet. Then I rounded up them horses and pointed them south till I found a buyer. Rancher down near a little one-horse town took them off my hands. But I had to throw in the buckskin."

"You mean you sold that buckskin?" Hayden asked, keeping one eye peeled for the rest of Hoffer's men.

"It was either that or no deal," Martin said. "That buckskin caught his eye the first thing. Besides, it was the roan that came back that night when I needed him."

"You could have used me," Hayden muttered. "I wasn't there either."

"You're here now," Martin said. "You got back a little too early to suit me. I was hoping you'd wait for me."

"I was afraid it might be a long wait," Hayden said. He glanced at Martin and added, "I wasn't sure you'd make it back at all."

Martin frowned. "Them boys thought they killed me, Buck. I couldn't let them have that on their conscience for the rest of their lives, could I?"

"So you decided to come back and kill them to keep their conscience from bothering them?"

Martin nodded. "I figgered it would ease their conscience considerable. Then they wouldn't have to regret what they'd done anymore."

Hayden grinned, studying the tall lean man with obvious affection. "Who gave you that haircut, Frank?"

"It was self-inflicted," Martin said, putting his old hat back on.

"That's what I figured. Still, it ain't a bad job for a mustanger."

"Well, I never set out to be no barber anyway," Martin said. "After I got rid of them horses I stopped at a barbershop, the only one in that town. But when I saw how drunk that barber was I figgered I'd better cut my own hair. A drunk barber can do more damage than a scalp-hungry Comanche."

He glanced at Mead, the coolness returning to his eyes. "Buck, it looks like you went and give my guns to this here greenhorn before I was even cold in my grave, and it appears he's already lost that old

Starr pistol I set such store by."

"I just loaned them to him," Hayden grunted. "I never meant for him to lose them."

"Well, that's what happens when you rely on a greenhorn," Martin said. "I won't ask why you brung him along in the first place."

"I did it as a favor," Hayden replied. "You know how them folks from back East are. They want to see what it's like out here. I thought I'd show him."

"Well, I hope you don't bring any more of them out here," Martin said. "I'm beginning to think maybe Hoffer didn't have such a bad idea after all. This country's too crowded already." He gave Mead another cool glance. "And it's getting too crowded around here for my taste. Think I'll take me a little walk and see what I can find. Might even find that old Starr pistol. This one ain't used to my hand yet."

"Better keep a eye peeled," Hayden said quietly. "There's still a couple of them left. Tony Bick and about one more, by my count."

"I was hoping you'd save Bick for me," Martin said.

He went back toward the tall rock, bent down and picked up the dead man's hat, tried it on, then reluctantly tossed it aside and bent down near Slim to repeat the ritual. He shook his head sadly as he faded into the rocks, wearing his own hat.

"I thought you said he didn't talk much," Mead said.

Hayden was reloading his guns and the empty loops in his belt and cartridges from the box Martin had brought him. He glanced the way Martin had gone and said in a low voice, "He usually don't. But just as sure as I tell someone that, even if he don't hear me, he seems to know what I said and then he starts talking his head off just to make me out a liar. He's always pulling stunts like that."

"He don't seem much worried about Bick and them," Mead observed. "Or whoever's left."

Hayden glanced uneasily at the rocks. "I don't think he's worried enough about them. The two he got weren't expecting him. Bick and that other one will be."

Mead was silent a moment. "Maybe you should have gone with him."

Hayden scowled. "I guess he figured you needed protection more than he does. And he wants a chance at Bick."

Mead remembered that he had not yet reloaded the shotgun, and did so now, while Hayden watched with no admiration in his pale eyes.

Several shots roared in the rocks in the direction Martin had gone. Then, after a moment of silence, Martin called in a strange voice, "Watch out, Buck. The little bastard snuck up on me again, then cut and ran. He may be coming your way."

"Come on," Hayden muttered. "And keep that scattergun handy."

Hayden led the way at a fast trot directly toward the sound of Martin's voice. Mead, keeping close behind him, was surprised at the big man's apparent recklessness.

"Hadn't we better take it easy?" he asked. "We're liable to run right into them."

"Except they ain't coming this way," Hayden grunted. "Not till they finish him. He only said that to keep us out of it. He's hoping to get them before he cashes in."

After that Mead followed in silence, his scared eyes darting in every direction, his heart pounding, a cold sick dread in his guts.

A gun roared just ahead of them. Then Martin called in an alarmed voice, "Watch out, Buck! They're still up there in them rocks!"

Hayden ran straight on without replying. A gun blasted from the rocks above and Hayden sprayed the slope with lead from his Winchester, working the lever and firing from the hip as he ran.

Mead saw Frank Martin lying on the ground behind a rock just ahead and he was beginning to think they would make it unscathed. Then something smashed into his shoulder and spun him around. Hayden grabbed him as he was falling and dragged him behind the rock where Martin lay, then turned his anxious attention to the wounded mustanger.

"You hit bad, Frank?"

"Bad enough. It looks like he got me good this time."

"Yeah, it looks like it," Hayden agreed, gazing with wide shocked eyes at the blood staining Martin's black coat. Yet in a way he was almost relieved to see the blood flowing from the wound. Until then he had almost wondered if it was Frank's ghost and not Frank himself that had returned to wreak vengeance on Hoffer's men. It seemed odd and a bit unsettling to see a man walking around that you thought was dead. Hayden had half believed there was something supernatural in the resurrection. There had never been any real hope that it would last. Dead men usually returned to their graves after a while. And it was obvious that Frank would soon have to return to his. He knew it as well as Hayden did. The grayness of death—the real thing this time—was already creeping over his face.

Martin opened his mouth to say something, but was interrupted by a scream of terror from Mead.

"Hayden! Watch out!"

Hayden flung himself away from Martin and dropped the empty Winchester. He whipped out a Colt and began firing as he hit the ground, firing at Tony Bick and Big Nose Sam who stood side by side in their socks, their own guns spouting lead. But even before Hayden got off his first shot he heard Frank Martin's gun blasting and saw Tony Bick jerk as Frank's bullets tore the life out of him. So Hayden turned his gun on Big Nose and emptied it at the ugly man as Big Nose fell.

He got to his feet and went to make sure the two men were dead. He relieved Big Nose of Frank's old Starr, then came back to kneel beside Frank. "Guess they didn't want to die with their boots on."

"Maybe they thought they'd live longer without them, and it almost worked." Martin glanced at Mead and his eyes were no longer cold. "Looks like bringing that greenhorn along wasn't such a bad idea after all, Buck. I'm beginning to think we're the greenhorns."

"Looks that way," Hayden agreed with a faint smile.

Mead was also smiling, despite the pain in his shoulder.

"He might like to have this here like-new Smith & Wesson as a souvenir," Martin said, laying the gun aside. "I figgered you might like to keep that old shotgun and the Starr for old times' sake. I know how soft-headed and sentimental you are."

Hayden's eyes were a little damp. "I didn't know it showed."

Martin frowned. "Don't waste it on me. Just put me back in my grave and take another trip someplace. Sooner or later folks will be saying how old Frank Martin came back to get the men who killed him. When you hear them saying that, you'll know I'm smiling in my grave. But if I catch you sneaking around there with any flowers, I'll come back a real ghost the next time and haunt you for the rest of your natural life."

"Whatever you say, Frank."

"When you start shoveling the dirt out of that grave, don't stop till you find what Hoffer's men were looking for," Martin said. "I figgered sooner or later you'd get curious and dig it up to see if I was really in there."

"I planned to as soon as I got a chance," Hayden admitted.

"What I got out of them horses is in my saddlebags, if somebody ain't already stole the horse and all," Martin said. "I left that roan tied behind the shack. All of it together should be a start on that horse ranch we were always talking about, and now you've got that stallion for a stud. I may drop by now and then to see how you're doing, but I'll try to keep out of sight so as not to cause no alarm. Somebody might think I'm a ghost."

Chapter 18

Mead was able to walk back down to the old shack, and even carried the shotgun in his good hand. Hayden carried Frank Martin and carefully laid him out on the ground near the grave. He did a crude job of bandaging Mead's shoulder, using strips torn from the spare shirt Mead had brought. Then he saddled the bay and helped Mead into the saddle.

"You think you can make it home all right?" he asked.

"I think so," Mead said.

"Get your wife to doctor that shoulder for you and do a better job of bandaging it than I did, and I think it will be all right in a week or two," Hayden told him. "I don't think there's a doc in town. The last one they had took sick and died. But if he couldn't cure himself he probably couldn't have done you much good either. I think he was just a vet before he came west. Helen can probably do a better job than he could have." Hayden managed a faint grin. "I was almost hoping I'd be the one to get nicked, so she'd take care of me for a while."

Mead shrugged his good shoulder, then said, "I guess you'll come by to get your horse after you bury Frank."

"The horse is yours," Hayden said. "A man needs a good riding animal. He'll soon be getting a little old for the kind of riding I do at times, but he's just what a greenhorn like you needs."

"Thanks," Mead said. "But I don't know how I can pay you."

"You already have," Hayden answered. "You saved my hide up

137

there about twice, and if you hadn't warned us Frank might not have managed to plug Tony Bick before he died. But I've got a feeling he would have plugged him *after* he died if he didn't before."

Mead nodded, glancing uneasily at Martin's body. "I feel that way too." He was silent a moment. "I guess we'll go on to California as soon as I'm up to it. What about you? You plan on staying here?"

Hayden sighed as he glanced at the still body of his friend and then out across the bleak gray mesa. "No, I don't think so. I guess I'll come back sometime to visit Frank's grave. But I doubt if I'll stay. It just wouldn't be the same without him. I never was around here much anyway. Frank liked it here, but it got a little lonesome for me at times."

"That's the way he liked it, wasn't it?" Mead asked.

Hayden nodded. "Well, I guess he'll have the mesa all to himself now, except for them boys up there on the hill, and they ain't in no shape to bother him. I may decide to bury them before I leave, or I may just leave them for the buzzards. They've got to eat too, and they ain't too particular."

"Well," Mead said, lifting the reins, "if you're ever out California way, look us up."

Hayden grinned. "Don't be surprised if you see me ride up one of these days."

Mead waved as he rode off.

Hayden lifted a hand, then got to work. He carefully wrapped Frank's body in a blanket, then began shoveling the loose dirt out of the grave.

Rose Hoffer stepped around the corner of the shack, a stubby revolver in her hand. "While you're at it," she said, "dig one for yourself."

Hayden looked at her carefully, then went on shoveling out the loose dirt. She was radiant and beautiful in a hat with a chin strap, a brown coat and a gray riding skirt, but the coolness in her eyes discouraged romantic notions.

"I usually take off my hat in the presence of a lady," he said, "but not when they point guns at me."

She walked slowly toward him, keeping the gun trained on his chest. "I'm going to kill you," she said, "just like you killed my father."

"Hoffer dead?" Hayden asked without much interest.

"You should know," she said. "You killed him!"

Hayden went on with his work. Maybe if she got close enough he could knock the gun out of her hand with the shovel. But maybe he would not have to. "What makes you think I killed him?"

"Who else could have done it?"

"I imagine it was Frank Martin," Hayden replied. "He didn't tell me he did it, but I figure it was him, and I don't figure he'd mind if you knew it."

"Frank Martin's dead!" she said scornfully. "Everyone knows that."

"He is now," Hayden said. "That's him there in that blanket."

"I don't believe you!"

"Would you know Frank Martin if you saw him?" Hayden asked.

She hesitated, but only for a moment. "Yes, I think so. I only saw him once in town, but I'm sure I would know him if I saw him again. He was a tall man with a red beard."

Hayden stuck the shovel in the loose dirt, got out of the grave and pulled the blanket back so she could see Martin's face.

Her dark eyes widened a little and the gun in her hand wavered. "That's Frank Martin," she said. "But I don't understand. I thought he was already dead."

Hayden put the blanket back over Martin's face. "That's what everyone thought. That's what he wanted them to think. He dug that grave himself so they wouldn't be looking for him before he was ready. The bullet just glanced off the side of his head."

"Those fools!" Rose said scornfully. "They could not do anything right!"

"Well, they got the job done this time," Hayden said heavily. "Not that it will do them much good."

"Did you kill them all?" she asked.

He nodded and started back to the grave, and Rose Hoffer fired. For a fleeing moment he wondered at the frightened look in her wide dark eyes, and then he dived to the ground and rolled into the grave, drawing his own gun as he did so.

Hoke Kelsey stood at the corner of the house with a gun in his hand, gazing down in disbelief at the blood pouring from the hole in his belly. Then he raised his scowling bearded face to glare at Rose Hoffer, who seemed even more horrified than Kelsey at what she had done. The big man raised his gun to fire, but at the last moment shifted it toward Hayden. He was like that when Hayden shot him in the Adam's apple.

Hoke tried to pull the old shack down with him as he fell.

"That man sure takes a lot of killing," Hayden complained as he climbed out of the grave. "Me and that greenhorn both thought we killed him up there this morning. But it seems like nobody wants to stay dead anymore." He glanced uneasily toward the rocky hill and added, "I think as soon as I get Frank buried I'll get the hell out of here before any of them others take a notion to come down here."

Rose Hoffer hesitated, watching him. "Which way are you going?"

He shrugged. "Doesn't really matter. I was sort of thinking about California. Maybe start a little horse ranch someplace out there."

Rose Hoffer smiled a little. "I like horses," she said.

Hayden watched her silently a moment, then holstered his gun and went back to work in the grave. "Well, I guess you can raise horses or cattle or whatever you want, now that Hoffer's dead. There's no one to stop you."

"Oh, I cannot stay here now," she said. "He did not own any of that land, and he sold most of his cattle. The people who were here before didn't own the land either, but now they may come back when they hear he's dead. I don't want to be here when they come."

Hayden glanced at the gun in her hand, and she put the gun back in her coat pocket. "I guess I was wrong about you, Hayden," she said. "I mean, about you killing my stepfather. I don't care about the others, but I'm glad you did not kill him."

"So am I," Hayden said, watching her. "How would you like to go to California?"

"I would love to," she said, smiling.

Hayden had the odd notion that under the blanket Frank Martin was also smiling.

Excerpt from
The Return of Frank Graben
by Van Holt

Molly Wilkins saw him shortly after sunrise that morning, sitting his blue
roan on the barren rocky slope above the Wilkins shack. A tall man in black,
with a bleak weathered face and cold gray eyes narrowed to glittering slits.

The girl ran screaming to the shack. "He's come back! It's Frank Graben! He's come back!"

Her fat stolid mother was cooking breakfast at the fireplace. "Hush, girl.
Don't talk nonsense. Frank Graben is dead."

"It's him, I tell you!" the excited girl cried. "Look up there on that ridge!"

Mrs. Wilkins looked out the window. "There's no one up there. You only
thought you saw someone. Now wash your hands and help me get breakfast
ready."

Homer Wilkins sat up on the plank bed, yawning and rubbing his eyes.
"What's all the fuss about? Can't a man get no sleep around here?"

His wife shot him a hard look. "It's time you was up and doin' anyway,
Homer Wilkins. What's to become of us the good Lord only knows."

Homer Wilkins sat on the edge of the bed in his patched overalls and
faded red underwear. "Now don't you set in on me again, Hettie," he said
placidly, while he contemplated a big toe that protruded from a hole in his
sock. "You know how my back hurts from sleepin' on that hard bed."

"Pa, I saw Frank Graben up on the ridge," Molly said.

"Hush, girl," Mrs. Wilkins said. "You know Frank Graben is dead."

"I tell you it was him!" the girl insisted. "Or his ghost!"

"Don't talk foolishness. I've told you time and again—"

"Hold on, Hettie," Wilkins said, and looked at his daughter. "We don't know for a fact he's dead. Ain't nobody seen his body. The man you saw, Molly—what kind of horse was he ridin'?"

"That blue roan! And it was Frank Graben! I know it was him!"

"I didn't see anyone," Mrs. Wilkins said. "Molly's got too much imagination, like I've said before."

"Well, there's only one way to find out," Homer Wilkins said, pulling on his boots. "I'm goin' to town."

"Any excuse not to do no work around here," Mrs. Wilkins said bitterly.

It was midmorning when Frank Graben rode down Hackamore's short dusty street, which at this hour was deserted. The whole town looked deserted. He studied the frame and adobe buildings with sharp gray eyes as he rode past. At the lower end of the street he reined in before the livery stable. As he swung down a stout, potbellied man came out and watched him with silent hostility.

Graben gave the man a cold glance. "You don't seem too surprised to see me."

"I figgered you'd be back," Barney Ludlow said in a harsh, bitter tone. "It ain't easy to kill a disease."

"You better keep that in mind," Graben said as he slung his saddlebags and blanket roll over his shoulder.

"Don't think it's over," Ludlow warned him. "You can't kill a man like Whitey Barlow and get away with it. The Star hands will be comin' after you with a rope."

"They'll need more than a rope," Frank Graben said in a quiet, grim tone, and walked up the street to the hotel.

The man behind the desk had seen him ride past the hotel and had time to compose himself. Yet his pale face glistened with sweat, and reminded Graben of a tree from which the bark had just been stripped. Sam Dauber kept his eyes lowered and remained silent as he pushed the register toward the tall man in black and watched him sign his name.

Graben laid the pen down and glanced at Dauber's sweaty face. "Things have sure changed," he observed, with his dark brows slightly raised and his gray eyes still narrowed to cold slits.

Dauber still did not say anything and did not look at him. He just handed Graben a key with the room number written on the attached tag.

Graben carried his blanket roll and saddlebags up to his room on the second floor. It was the same room he had had before, overlooking the narrow street. There was an iron bedstead with a lumpy mattress and clean sheets, a bureau with a mirror, a chest of drawers with a pitcher of water and a basin on top. Graben lowered his stuff to the floor, glanced through the window at the street, then took off his hat and washed his face and hands. Drying on a threadbare towel, he glanced at himself in the mirror and sighed.

He was not quite twenty-eight, but his bleak weathered face looked closer to thirty-five. There were permanent squint wrinkles around the hooded gray eyes—eyes so cold that few people could meet them without flinching. It would still have been a remarkably handsome face if he had smiled. But he never did, except in a wry, mocking way. The hair alone did not displease him. It was dark brown hair with a slight wave and reddish-copper glints.

He knocked the dust from his flat-crowned black hat and put it back on. Then he drew the double-action .41 Colt from his waistband, spun the cylinder and checked the loads. Tucking the gun back in his waistband, he opened the door and went down the stairs, a tall lean man, as graceful on his feet as he was in the saddle.

He gave Sam Dauber a narrow glance as he passed the desk but Dauber was careful not to look at him, lest Graben see the dislike and resentment in his dull eyes. Outside, Graben tramped along the boardwalk and pushed in through the swing doors of the Last Chance Saloon. There was no one in the saloon except for the man behind the bar. Without waiting to be asked, the man set out a bottle and a glass. His face had the same wooden expression, the same look of dull hostility and resentment Graben had seen on the faces of Sam Dauber and Barney Ludlow.

Graben poured himself a drink, lit a thin black cigar and looked at the saloonkeeper through slitted eyes. "Things have sure changed," he said.

Max Rumford slowly raised his bloodshot eyes and looked at Graben with hatred. He looked like a red-eyed bull getting set to charge, but he only said softly, "Maybe not as much as you think."

A horse trotted long the street, saddle leather creaked and a moment later a swarthy man with a dirty brown mustache pushed in through the batwing doors. His sleepy dark eyes widened in surprise when he saw Graben. Then the mustache curved away from yellow teeth in a cheerful grin. "Hello, Frank," Lum Mulock said as he stepped up to the bar. "I heard you was dead."

"Oh?" Graben said coolly. "Where did you hear that?"

Mulock grinned and scratched his dimpled chin. "I heard it somewheres."

He glanced at the birdshead Colt in Graben's waistband. "Where are them Russian pistols you had, Frank?"

"As you may recall, I hardly ever wear them."

Mulock was grinning at him out of the corners of his eyes. "Seems like I saw somebody else wearin' them."

"If you see him wearing them again," Graben said, "tell him to get ready."

"Ready for what?"

"A hotter climate," Graben said.

Lum Mulock's eyes brightened with interest. He tasted his drink and smacked his lips with relish. "Rube and the boys will be real pleased to hear you're back," he said. "Things have been a lot more peaceful around here since you killed Whitey Barlow."

"Except for one thing," Graben said. "I didn't kill him."

"That a fact?" Mulock's grin got even broader, showing his meaty red lips as well as his crooked yellow teeth. "Wonder why ever'body around here thinks it was you."

"I guess somebody put the idea in their heads," Graben said, watching Mulock with cold narrow eyes.

Mulock wiped his mouth with the back of a dirty brown hand. "It was a easy idea for them to believe," he said. "Ever'body knows how you and old Whitey hated each other at first sight."

That, Graben had to admit, was not so far from the truth, and he found himself thinking about that cold windy day five months before when he had first seen Whitey Barlow.

Graben had stopped at a waterhole in what seemed to him the middle of nowhere, over near the eastern edge of that vast desert plain surrounded by barren gray mountains. It had been days since he had passed a town or even a house, and he had not known there was a ranch anywhere around, although there were some old cow tracks near the waterhole. Then the five riders had come up out of an arroyo two hundred yards away and cantered toward him in a cloud of dust. They must have spotted him at a distance and waited for him in the arroyo, or he would have seen them or their dust earlier. That thought made him uneasy and he was not reassured by the rapid, businesslike manner of their approach.

Yet he took his time about filling his canteen and hanging it back on the saddle horn. Then he stood beside his horse and his slitted gray eyes watched the group as they charged up and halted, looking them over with a cool reserve.

The man in the lead was a white-haired man in his late forties or early fifties, a tall gaunt man with icy blue eyes and a face tanned to old leather. The rider beside him was just as tall, and more strongly built. He had dark eyes and a strong face covered with black beard, and he was a good twenty years younger than the white-haired man.

It was the white-haired man who asked in a sharp, rude tone, "What are you doing here?"

"Watering my horse," Graben said.

"This is my water," the white-haired man said. "Move along."

Graben did not like the man's tone or his manner. "This your land?" he asked.

The white-haired man blinked once, as if surprised by the question. There was the slightest hesitation before he replied. "As far as you're concerned, it is."

"Not good enough," Graben said. "Unless you can show me a deed to this land, you can go to hell."

The black-bearded fellow's dark eyes hardened with a look of anger. "Mister, this here's Star range," he snapped.

"I'll do the talking, Graf," Whitey Barlow said, his eyes still on Graben. "You've got a lot to learn about this country, mister."

"I know all about this country," Graben said flatly as he stepped into the saddle, never taking his narrow eyes off the five men. "And I know all about men like you. You probably don't even own the ground you roost on, yet you think you've got some God-given right to all the range you may ever want or need and nobody else can ride across it without your permission. Well, I'll repeat what I said a minute ago. You can go to hell." He deliberately ran his cool eyes over all five of them and added, "You can all go to hell for all I care."

Graf's chest tightened with anger, and his hand started toward his gun.

"If you touch that gun I'll kill you," Graben said in a soft, deadly tone. "And then I'll kill Whitey."

"Hold it, Graf," Whitey said harshly, his pale eyes glowing with anger. "I know how to handle men like him." Then he spoke directly to Graben. "Mister, I advise you to turn around and head back the way you came. What lies between these mountains is all Star range, and you won't find no welcome in my town. I'll make sure of that."

"Oh, you own the town too?" Graben said dryly.

After a moment the man slowly nodded. "You'll think I do, if you try to go there. You'll think I own the town and everybody in it."

With that he reined his horse around and rode back the way he had come, and Graf and the others reluctantly followed, looking back over their shoulders at Graben.

Watching them ride off, Graben had seriously considered following Whitey Barlow's advice and heading back over the mountains the way he had come. He knew that would be the smart thing to do. But there was nothing back that way worth going back to, and it was not in him to run from trouble.

After about a minute he had ridden on in exactly the same direction he had intended to go all along, which was almost in the same direction that the Star men had gone. And as he walked and trotted his horse out across that mountain-rimmed desert plain, he watched those five men draw slowly away from him, heading northwest. But after a while one of them left the others and headed straight west, and somehow Frank Graben knew that one was on his way to the town Whitey had mentioned.

On the outskirts of the town, several hours later, Graben met the rider heading back the way he had come. They met and passed without speaking, the Star hand scowling darkly, Graben watching him with cool eyes, deliberately turning his head to watch the man ride off and to let him know he did not trust him behind his back—a deliberate insult that was not missed by the Star hand glaring around to watch him also.

Then the blue roan was walking along the dusty street, and Graben turned his attention to the silent, deserted-looking town. When he reined in before the stable and started to dismount, Barney Ludlow came out, looked him over with hard eyes and spoke in a harsh flat tone that might have been borrowed from Whitey Barlow himself.

"Keep moving. I don't want your business."

Graben relaxed in the saddle and watched the short, potbellied man in silence for a moment. Then he asked, "Do you own this place, or does that rancher?"

Barney Ludlow's eyes were mean, his voice as harsh as before. "Whitey Barlow is a good friend of mine," he said. "If it wasn't for the Star Ranch there wouldn't be a town here. And you'll find everybody in Hackamore feels the same way I do."

After a moment Graben silently turned his horse and rode back along the street to see if that was true. At the only restaurant he reined in, dismounted, tied his horse and went inside. Behind the counter stood a gray-haired woman with a wrinkled face who might have been Whitey Barlow's sister. Graben sat down at a table and said, "Get anything to eat around here?"

She looked at him with hard eyes and asked, "You the one had that run-in with Whitey Barlow?"

Graben silently nodded, his eyes cold.

"Then you better keep moving," the woman said. "We don't want your kind around here."

Graben thought about that for a moment. "My kind?"

"You know what I mean," the woman said, looking out the window at the empty street as if she expected to see Whitey Barlow and his men riding into town.

"I'm not sure I do," Graben said. "Maybe you'd better tell me."

The woman looked at him with scorn. Then, without another words, she went into the kitchen in back and slammed the door. Graben sat there for a few minutes, but somehow he knew that he could wait there forever and the woman would not come back out until he left. So he got up and went back out to his horse. He untied the horse and led him across the dusty street to the hotel, while Sam Dauber watched apprehensively through the window. The hotel man's face was drenched with sweat by the time Graben opened the door and entered the lobby.

Dauber was already shaking his head, a scared but stubborn look in his eyes, as Graben approached the desk. "I'm sorry, mister," he said in an unsteady voice, "but we ain't got no rooms for rent."

Showing no surprise, Graben thumbed his hat back on his head. "What about something to eat, then?" he asked.

Again the man shook his head, almost desperately. He took out a handkerchief and mopped his face. "It's too late for lunch and we don't serve supper till six." He fumbled for his watch and looked at it. "That's nearly four hours from now."

"I guess I'll just have to come back then," Graben said dryly.

"It won't do no good," Dauber said. "We only serve our guests and regulars who eat here all the time. It's a hotel policy."

For a time Graben regarded the man in silence, and Dauber could not meet his cold gray eyes. Then Graben turned away and went out to the veranda and sat down in one of the chairs, his weathered face blank as he looked along the deserted street. He was trying to decide what to do.

For some time now there had been a feeling in his gut that he was going to die. He did not know how or when, but instead of going away as expected, the feeling had got worse until he could no longer ignore it. He had started being more careful, had even gone out of his way on several occasions to avoid trouble. And he had come here, to this remote place, looking for peace. Instead of finding it, he had just found more trouble.

He knew what he should do. He should ride on. He also knew he would not do it. Not now. He couldn't, being the kind of man he was. Whitey Barlow and the people of this town had made that impossible.

He glanced at the blue roan standing at the rail. Though tired from long travel, the gelding had his head raised, his bright dark eyes watching Graben expectantly. When Graben left the horse tied at a hitchrail it usually meant that he would be riding on in a few minutes. Otherwise he would put the horse in the nearest stable or corral and see that he was properly cared for.

Graben got to his feet, stepped off the porch, untied the horse and led him down the street to the Last Chance Saloon.

The red-faced, heavyset bartender with gray hair curling about his ears watched through bloodshot eyes as Graben came in through the swing doors.

Graben dug a coin out of his pocket and laid it on the bar. "Whiskey," he said.

The saloonkeeper smiled a tiny humorless smile. "Fresh out," he said.

Graben glanced at the bottles lined up on the back bar. Then, silently, he drew the birdshead Colt from his waistband and placed it on the bar near the saloonkeeper.

Max Rumford's bloodshot eyes rested on the gun for a long moment. "That thing supposed to scare me?" he asked.

"Did I hear you say you were fresh out of whiskey?"

Rumford nodded. "That's right."

"Well, if you ain't you soon will be," Graben said quietly, and lifting the gun he calmly and unhurriedly shattered four of the full bottles on the back bar. Then, while the whiskey still ran off the back bar and dripped to the floor, he looked at the red-eyed saloonkeeper and said, "One left."

Rumford did not move for a long moment. It seemed that he had even quit breathing. The bloodshot eyes watched Graben with hatred. Then he slowly took a bottle and a glass from the back bar and poured Graben a drink. He silently watched him drink the whiskey and made no move to pick up the coin.

Leaving the coin on the bar, Graben thrust his gun back into his waistband and said, "You can charge the damage to Whitey Barlow." Then he went out and Rumford's bloodshot eyes followed him like red bullets.

The preceding was from the gritty western novel
The Return of Frank Graben

To keep reading, click or go here:
http://amzn.to/1eeiDpk

The Revenge of Tom Graben

Frank Graben stopped his blue roan gelding among some rocks on a bleak barren ridge top and studied the country around him with his gray eyes narrowed to glittering slits. His face was bony and darkly weathered. His dark hair had a copper tinge. He wore a flat-crowned black hat, a double-breasted black shirt and black trousers. There was a brown corduroy coat tied behind his saddle. He packed his Smith & Wesson .44 Russian pistols in tied-down holsters.

There were enemies looking for him, and he had no friends anywhere. He kept to himself and there was something about him that kept most people at a distance. Those who ventured closer were usually looking for trouble, and they usually found it.

Two days before at dusk he had stopped at a place called Turley's, a combination store and saloon. Several bearded, rough-garbed men stood at the bar drinking when Graben came in through the swing doors and stopped near the front end of the bar to drink a beer in silence. He did not appear to notice the men but he was aware that they were sizing him up in the back-bar mirror and grinning at one another in a way that spelled trouble. So he finished his beer and went through a doorway into the store to get a sack of grub and a few other things he needed.

When he came back out the five men had left the saloon and were standing outside, near his horse. They were still grinning but there was nothing friendly in their grins. Graben went around them and tied the grub sack to the horn of his saddle in frowning silence, then stepped into the saddle.

"Where'd you get that horse, mister?" one of them said then. It was the youngest of the five, a beardless boy still in his teens.

Graben merely stared at him through cold narrowed eyes and did not bother to answer. A couple of the others took a closer look at him and shifted their feet uncomfortably, perhaps sensing that he was nobody to fool around with. But the kid saw only himself and he liked what he saw.

His voice rose a little. "I'm talkin' to you, mister! I said where did you get that horse?"

Graben still remained silent, watching the boy, watching them all, and it was plain by then that his unexpected silence was getting on their nerves.

The boy's voice was a little shrill as he said, "That there's my horse, mister! He was stole from me a while back!"

Graben merely lifted the reins and started to turn the roan, and as he did so the boy yelled something and went for his gun. A moment later he lay dead in the dirt and Graben's smoking revolver was trained on the others.

"Anybody else think I'm a horse thief?" he asked.

They eyed the gun uneasily and shook their heads.

Then, as Graben backed the horse across the road, still keeping them covered, one of them said, "I shore wouldn't want to be in yore place, mister. That was Tobe Unger's kid brother you killed."

Graben did not know who Tobe Unger was and he did not bother to ask, but he judged that he was somebody to reckon with, or thought he was, and would no doubt be coming after Graben as soon as he heard. And the men who had seen the shooting would be with him. If Graben did not miss his guess, they were already on his trail, and might even circle ahead to set up an ambush.

That was why he studied the old shack with care before riding down the rocky slope toward it. The shack was as weathered and gray as the rocks around it, and looked abandoned. No smoke rose from the rock chimney, there were no horses in the sagging pole corral, and the glassless windows were just empty shadowy holes, like eyes watching him.

For some reason, the place made him uneasy. But he decided he was just jumpy as a result of killing a boy who apparently had a mean, tough brother, and several friends who looked like pirates in western garb.

When he did approach the shack it was by circling down through the rocks and coming up on the shack's blind side, where there were no windows. He might have saved himself the trouble, for when he got inside he found wide cracks between the unchinked logs through which anyone in the one-room shack could have seen him. But there was no one inside the shack and it did not appear that there had been anyone here for some time. The rough plank floor was covered with dust and debris and the stone fireplace was about the same, a good indication that it had not been used recently.

Graben went back outside to the well and drew up the wooden bucket on its frayed, half-rotten rope. There was no water in the bucket. It was half full of sand.

A piercing cackle caused him to drop the bucket and spin around, whipping out a gun. A woman had just emerged from the rocks leading a saddled horse. The sun was directly in Graben's slitted eyes and he could not tell whether the woman's sun-cured face was young or old, whether her hair was gray or sun-bleached blond. But he could tell that she was laughing at him.

"Ain't no water in that well, mister," she said, limping toward him.

"Ain't been for years."

Graben's narrow eyes studied the rocks behind her, and seeing this she cackled again and said, "Don't worry, I'm by myself, more's the pity. Nobody wants nothin' to do with Crazy Cora."

She sat down on the ground, tugged off her right boot and rubbed her foot with a callused hand. Graben saw now that she was somewhere in her middle years, but he could not narrow it down much closer than that.

"My horse picked up a limp a piece back," she said with a rueful grin. "Now it looks like I've picked up one, too."

Graben remained silent and she glanced up to study his lean hard face and cold slitted eyes. "I got a place farther back in the hills," she said, hooking a thumb over her shoulder. "Sometimes I come over this way lookin' for strays. Stray men, that is."

She cackled again, but there was no trace of a smile in Graben's eyes. He had not wanted to run into anyone, much less a crazy, man-hunting old woman.

Turning away without a word, he went toward his horse.

"Hey, hold on a minute, mister," she said. "I didn't mean to alarm you. I ain't in the habit of ropin' and brandin' any of the men I see. I just try to find out if they've seen my daughter. She run off with that no-account Tobe Unger three months back and I ain't seen her since."

Graben stopped and turned to look at the woman and he was surprised to see that her faded eyes were damp. Perhaps she was not as crazy as she seemed. "Unger hang ground here much?" he asked.

"Not no more," she said bitterly. "He used to hang around my place all the time till he got my Gibby to run off with him."

"Gibby?"

Crazy Cora tugged off her other boot and massaged that foot also. "I just knowed it was gonna be a boy, and I was gonna name him Gib after his no-account pa what done run off on me. Only it weren't no him, and I named *her* Gibby. Purtiest baby I ever did see and she just got purtier and purtier as she growed up. All I could do to keep men away from her. Wouldn't never allow no men around there on account of her. But that no-account Tobe Unger tricked me, when I should of knowed what he was after. He let on like he was sweet on me, when all he wanted was to use my place for a hideout for him and his gang and to sweet-talk my Gibby behind my back. He ever comes back around, I aim to empty my shotgun at him."

She gestured toward her horse and Graben saw the gun in the saddle scabbard.

"Don't reckon you've seen anything of them?" she asked. "Gibby's a towhead with light green eyes and the cutest baby face you ever saw. Sometimes it don't seem rightly possible that she could be my girl. She's just seventeen and Tobe Unger's more'n twice that, and a big ugly mean-lookin' rascal. What a girl like her ever saw in him I don't know. Course, in my case there weren't too many men to pick and choose from. But Gibby could of had any man she wanted, and someday the right one would of turned up, and I wouldn't of run him off like I did the others. I kept tellin' her that. Just be patient a while longer, I told her. Don't run off with the first sweet-talkin' rascal that comes along like I did. You'll live to regret it if you do.

"But I never thought to warn her about Tobe Unger, and I sure never thought about him pullin' the wool over my eyes the way he did neither. I knowed he was mean as a snake, but I thought it was all out in the open. He just never seemed to me like the cunnin' type, and when he made such a fuss over my Gibby I just thought it was all in good-natured fun and that he was tryin' to cheer her up 'cause the pore girl always seemed so lonesome without nobody her own age around to talk to. But I guess I should of knowed what he was after all along."

Graben stood by his horse with the reins in his hand, a look of growing impatience in his eyes. He felt sorry for the old woman in a general way, but there was nothing he could do for her, and he did not have time to listen to her troubles. He had his own to worry about, and every moment he remained here increased his danger.

"I haven't seen anyone who looked like your daughter," he said. Then he asked, "Maybe you could tell me where's the nearest water?"

"The nearest water," she said, "is at my place."

Crazy Cora's place turned out to be only a few miles away, and she decided that her horse's feet were in better shape to walk that distance than her own were. En route she explained to Graben that she and "Gib" had squatted on the only sweet waterhole around right after they were married and had hauled logs from mountains thirty miles away to build their one-room cabin, later adding a lean-to kitchen. But in spite of this addition the house turned out to be only a fraction larger than the shack they had just left, and Graben wondered, but did not ask, how they had all managed to crowd into the place when the Unger gang was around. Where had two women and half a dozen men slept? Perhaps the men had slept outside.

The house and waterhole were in a little pocket surrounded by brushy, rocky hills. The area was littered with rocks and boulders that had tumbled down, and Crazy Cora sat down on a nearby rock and watched Graben as he squatted down to fill his canteen while his horse drank beside him. When the woman suddenly let out one of her startling, unexpected cackles, he raised his head and looked at her through cold half-lidded eyes, wondering again if she was as crazy as her nickname implied.

"I was just thinkin' about the look on your face over there when you drawed up that bucket of sand," she said. "What's your name anyway? I know a body ain't supposed to ask, but you don't have to give me your real name. I'd just like to know something to call you when I tell folks about runnin' into you over there and that look on your face."

"Why don't you just make one up for me?" Graben suggested.

She studied him for a moment and then said, "I think I'll call you Graben."

Graben gave her a startled glance. "Why Graben?"

"You remind me of a fellow named Graben who come through here a few months back," she said, again studying his face. "In some ways he looked a lot like you. Tall like you, same color of hair. I think his eyes was more blue than yours. I guess you'd call yours gray, wouldn't you?"

"I would. Some people call them blue."

He pulled his horse back from the water and hung his canteen on the horn. His back to Crazy Cora, he asked, "You happen to catch his first name?"

"Seems like it was Tom," she said. "Yeah, that's what it was, Tom Graben."

Graben had started to tighten his cinch. Now he loosened it again and sat down on a rock not far from Crazy Cora. "That fellow happen to say where he was headed?"

"He never said," Crazy Cora told him. "But it don't matter none, 'cause he never got there, wherever it was."

Graben glanced at her leathery face and bright pale eyes. "What makes you think that?" he asked in the same idle tone as before.

Crazy Cora's own voice dropped to a conspiratorial whisper. "I never meant to tell nobody, but now I don't care who knows about it. They killed him, Tobe and the others did. They thought he was some kind of law snoopin' around, so they killed him."

Graben was prepared for that and there was no change on his bleak weathered face. He showed nothing more than idle curiosity. "Fair fight?"

There was utter scorn in Crazy Cora's pale eyes. "Nah! He looked plumb dangerous, that one did. Them pale cold blue eyes could look right through you and send a chill down your spine. So they didn't take no chances. Shot him down from behind as he started to get on his horse, that fine buckskin Dub Astin still rides. They played poker for his horse and saddle and his guns. Dub got the horse and saddle and Zeke Fossett got the guns."

Frank Graben sat on the rock thinking about what the woman had told him. So Tom was dead, he thought. Tom had been two years older than Frank, and more of a man than he would ever be, but a loner like himself. As boys growing up back in Missouri they had been close, but they had had their differences and had gone their separate ways after their parents died and the farm was sold. Frank had not seen or heard from Tom since, and now he would never see him again.

"Funny thing though," he heard Crazy Cora say. "They took his body back up in the hills yonder and just left him there. A few days later they got to thinkin' maybe they should of hid the body better and went back up there to do the job right. But they never did find him. It was night when they took him up there and left him and it had come a big rain so there wasn't no tracks they could foller back to where they was before. We never could figger out whether they just couldn't find where they left him, or whether somebody had rode by the next day and decided to take him into Rock Crossin' or someplace and bury him decent. We kept expectin' to hear something about it, but we never did, and you can believe we never asked nobody about it."

"No, I guess not," Frank Graben grunted, his eyes unbelievably cold. As cold, Crazy Cora was thinking, as Tom Graben's eyes.

Frank got to his feet and glanced at the unpainted log house. "Anybody else here that night?"

"Mac Radner was here, playin' cards with Tobe and them." She hooked a thumb over her shoulder. "Mac and his two brothers has got them a little place back over here a piece. They call theirselves horse ranchers, but they stole most of them horses. And sometimes they ride with Tobe and the boys if they're wanted or needed."

"Well, I better push on," Graben said, going toward his horse.

Crazy Cora went to her own horse and casually pulled the double barrel shotgun from the scabbard. Graben watched her uneasily, but she made no threatening gesture with the gun and he assumed that she meant to take it inside after he left. "No call to rush off," she said. "I aim to rustle up some chuck here before long, and I might even let you spend the night, if you was lonesome for a little company."

Her sudden cackle made him wince. "I'm not that lonesome," he said, scowling, and stepped into the saddle. "Thanks for the water."

Crazy Cora merely nodded, silent for a change, and watched him turn his horse to ride off. She noticed that he was heading back the way they had come a little earlier, but she did not think anything about it.

She watched him until he was almost out of range, and then she brought up the sawed-off shotgun and fired both barrels at his back, aiming high enough not to hit the horse. Crazy Cora liked horses, but she had no use for men who had no use for her.

She saw the stranger slump forward in the saddle, but somehow he hung on and got the horse into a gallop along the narrow winding valley through which the trail ran.

"He won't git far!" Crazy Cora shrieked, dancing with glee. "Crazy Cora can do it just as good as Tobe and them! I'd go after him, Bess, if you wasn't all gimpy like me!"

Frank Graben did not know how he managed to stay in the saddle, or how far he rode. He was barely conscious most of the time. The horse slowed to a trot and then to a walk, and finally stopped, and he became dimly aware that four rough-looking men sat their horses before him, blocking the trail.

"Well, look who we got here," one of them said in a taunting, vaguely familiar voice. "Tobe is gonna be real pleased when he finds out we done got the man what killed Chip."

"Looks like Crazy Cora already put some buckshot in him," another chuckled.

"Hell, let's finish the bastard and get it over with," said a third.

He could not see their faces clearly, because the light was fading and he could not get his eyes into proper focus for some reason. But now he knew who they were, and he knew they meant to kill him. His hand groped for his gun and found the butt, but the gun seemed to weigh a ton and he did not have the strength to lift it.

Then all four of them were shooting into him and he was falling from the saddle.

A tall man stood up in the rocks on the rough slope above Graben and began firing, the dark long-barreled pistol bucking in his fist. Two of the riders tumbled out of their saddles and the other two turned their horses and spurred away. The tall man in the rocks fired one shot after them and then his gun clicked on an empty chamber.

A minute later Frank Graben found the tall man bending over him. He peered up into the lean weathered face and cold pale blue eyes of Tom Graben. And that gaunt stubbled face was the last thing Frank Graben saw before he died.

The preceding was from the gritty western novel
The Revenge of Tom Graben

To keep reading, click or go here:
http://amzn.to/1c9lT7s

Excerpt from
Rebel With A Gun
by Van Holt

On a gray, drizzly day in the spring of 1865, a tall slender young man on a brown horse rode along the muddy street of Hayville, Missouri. Several heads turned to stare at him, but he seemed not to notice anyone, and he did not stop in the town, but rode on out to a weather-beaten, deserted-looking house and dismounted in the weed-grown yard.

At the edge of the yard there was a grave surrounded by a low picket fence and he went that way and stood with his head bared in the slow drizzle and stared at the grave with bleak, bitter blue eyes. He was only nineteen but looked thirty. He had been only fifteen when the war started. That seemed like a lifetime ago, another world —a world that had been destroyed. All that was left was a deserted battlefield, a devastated wasteland swarming with scavengers and pillagers.

An old black man with only one eye appeared from a dripping pine thicket and slowly reached up to remove a battered hat and scratch the white fuzz on his head.

"Dat you, Mistuh Ben?"

"It's me, Mose," Ben Tatum said.

"I knowed sooner or later you'd come back to see yo' ma's grave. She died two years back now. Never was the same aftuh we heard the news about yo' pa. And too she was worried sick about you. Is it true you rode with Quantrill, Mistuh Ben?"

"You can hear anything, Mose."

"Yessuh, dat's de truth, it sho' is. But I wouldn't rightly blame you if you did. Dem Yankees sho' did raise hell, didn't they, Mistuh Ben?"

Old Mose was something of a diplomat. Had he been talking to a Yankee, he would have said it was the Rebels who had raised hell.

Or he might have said it was Quantrill's raiders.

"The war's over, Mose."

"Yessuh, I sho' do hope so, I sho' do." Old Mose reached up and rubbed his good eye, and for a moment his blind eye seemed to peer at the tall young man in the old coat. "But folks say there's some who still ain't surrendered and don't plan to. I hear there ain't no amnesty for Quantrill's men. Is dat true, Mistuh Ben?"

"That's what I heard, Mose."

"Dat sho' is too bad. I guess dat mean there still be ridin' and shootin' and burnin' just like befo'."

"Maybe not, Mose."

"I sho' do hope not. Has you only got one gun, Mistuh Ben? I hear some of Quantrill's men carry fo' or five all at one time."

Ben Tatum glanced down at the double-action Cooper Navy revolver in his waistband. He buttoned his coat over the gun. "I just got in the habit of carrying this one, Mose. I wouldn't feel right without it."

"Guess a man can't be too careful dese days." Old Mose thoughtfully rubbed the wide bridge of his nose, his good eye wandering off down the road toward Hayville. "Well, I just come by to check on yo' ma's grave. She sho' was a fine woman. Mistuh Snyder down to de bank own de place now. I guess you heard his boy Cal done gone and married dat Farmer girl you was sweet on?"

Ben Tatum let out a long sigh. "No, I hadn't heard, Mose. But it doesn't matter now. I can't stay here."

Old Mose looked like he had lost his only friend. "Where will you go, Mistuh Ben?"

"I don't know yet. West, maybe."

He turned and looked at the old house with its warped shingles and staring, broken windows. He did not go inside. He knew the house would be as empty as he felt.

He turned toward his horse.

"Oh, Mistuh Ben!"

"What is it, Mose?"

"I almost forgot," old Mose said, limping forward. "Yo' ma's sister, what live over to Alder Creek, she said if I ever saw you again to be sho' and tell you to come by and see her."

"All right, Mose. Thanks."

He thoughtfully reached into a pocket, found a coin and tossed it to the old Negro.

A gnarled black hand shot up and plucked the coin out of the air. "Thanks, Mistuh Ben. I sho' do 'preciate it. Times sho' is hard since they went and freed us darkies. Them Yankees freed us but they don't feed us."

He rode back through Hayville. The small town seemed all but deserted. But it had always seemed deserted on rainy days, and sometimes even on sunny days. But for some reason Ben Tatum could no longer recall very many sunny days. They had faded into the mist of time, the dark horror of war.

He stopped at a store to get a few supplies. The sad-eyed old man behind the counter seemed not to recognize him. But Ben Tatum had been only a boy when he had left, and now he was a tall young man with shaggy brown hair and a short beard. He had not shaved on purpose because he had no wish to be recognized. And he suspected that old man Hill did not recognize him on purpose. It was usually best not to recognize men who had ridden with Quantrill.

The slow rain had stopped, and when he left the store Ben Tatum saw a few people stirring about. A handsome, well-dressed young couple were going along the opposite walk. The young man had wavy dark hair and long sideburns, a neatly trimmed mustache. He wore a dark suit and carried a cane, like a dandy, and his arrogant face was familiar. The girl had long dark hair and just a hint of freckles. It was Jane Farmer. Only it would be Jane Snyder now. Cal Snyder had stayed here and courted her and married her while Ben Tatum was dodging bullets and sleeping out in the wet and cold, when he got a chance to sleep at all. Cal Snyder had not gone to the war. His father had hired a man to go in his place, a man who had not come back. He had been killed at Shiloh.

Ben Tatum stopped and stared at her as if a mule had kicked him in the belly. But neither Jane Snyder nor her dandified husband showed the slightest sign that they recognized him or even saw him. They went on along the walk and turned into the restaurant.

With a sick hollow feeling inside him, Ben Tatum got back in his wet saddle and rode on along the muddy street, returning to the bleak empty world from which he had come, homeless now and a wanderer forever. The war had taught him how to lose. Turn your back and ride off as if it did not matter. Never let the winners know you cared.

"Ben! Ben Tatum!"

For a fleeting moment hope rose up in him like an old dream returning. But then he realized that it was not her voice, and when he looked around he saw a fresh-faced girl just blooming into womanhood, a girl with long light brown hair that was almost yellow and a face that looked somehow familiar. She was smiling and radiant and seemed happy to see him. Puzzled, he searched his memory but failed to place her, and it made him uneasy. He lived in a world where it did not pay to trust your closest friends, much less strange beautiful girls who seemed too happy to see you. Many girls that age had been spies during the war and had lured many a dazzled man to their destruction. Some of them might still be luring men to their destruction, for the war still was not over for some men and never would be over. Men like Ben Tatum. And the fact that she knew his name proved nothing.

So he merely touched his hat and kept his horse at the same weary trot along the muddy street, and behind him he heard a little exclamation: "Well!" He rode on out of town, wondering who she was. He noticed that it had started raining again.

Alder Creek was a two-day ride west of Hayville. There were no streets in Alder Creek, just narrow roads that wound among the trees that grew everywhere, and most of the houses were scattered about in clearings that had been hacked out of the trees and brush.

Ben Tatum's aunt lived in a big old house on a shelf above the hidden murmuring creek that had given the town its name. Her husband had died years ago in a mysterious hunting accident and she had soon remarried and had a lively stepdaughter. Her two sons had died in the war and she had no other children of her own.

Cora Wilburn had been a slender, attractive woman in her late thirties the last time Ben Tatum had seen her. But the war had aged her as it had aged everyone else. There were lines in her tired face and streaks of gray in her hair, and she had put on weight. But she seemed glad to see him, and it was good to see a smiling, friendly face.

She hugged him and patted his back just the way his own mother would have done had she lived to see him come home. "My, you've sure grown into a tall, fine-looking man," she said, blinking away tears. Her voice sounded as old and tired as she looked. "But you need a haircut and some decent clothes. Sam's a pretty good barber, they tell me, and you can have some of Dave's clothes. He was tall like you. I appreciate the nice letter you sent me when Dave and Lot were killed."

He nodded, and just then he noticed a tall slender girl of about thirteen standing on the porch watching him with lively green eyes and a mischievous smile. "This can't be Kittie," he said in a slow surprise.

"Yes, that's Kittie," Cora Wilburn said in her tired voice. "Ain't she run up like a weed? Soon be grown. It's getting hard to keep the boys away from her or her away from the boys."

Kittie Wilburn gave her dark head a little toss and flashed her white teeth in a smile, but said nothing.

"Sam's at the barbershop," Cora Wilburn added. "Soon as you eat a bite and catch your breath, you should go on down there and get some of that hair cut off your head and face. I want to see what you look like without that beard."

Sam Wilburn was a strange, moody man, by turns silent and talkative. He had a habit of watching you out of the corners of cold green eyes, without ever facing you directly. He was trimming an old man's white hair when Ben Tatum opened the door of the small barbershop. He glanced up at him out of those strange green eyes and said, "Have a seat. I'll be with you in a few minutes."

Ben Tatum sat down in a chair against the wall and picked up an old newspaper. The war was still going on when the newspaper was printed, but Quantrill had already disappeared and was thought dead by them and his followers had scattered, some of them forming small guerrilla bands of their own, or degenerating into common outlaws and looters, preying on the South as well as the North. Others had gone into hiding or left the country. Few had any homes left to return to, even if it had been safe to go home.

When the old man left, Ben Tatum took his place in the barber's chair and Sam Wilburn went to work on his hair. He did not seem very happy to see the younger man. They had never had much use for each other, and now and then Ben Tatum had idly wondered if Sam Wilburn had arranged the hunting accident that had left Cora Medlow an attractive young widow. Why Cora had married Sam Wilburn was another mystery he still had not figured out. But the world was full of things he would probably never understand.

Sam Wilburn glanced through the window at a wagon creaking down the crooked, stump-dotted road that passed for the town's main street. "I've been wondering when you'd show up," he said. When Ben Tatum made no reply, he asked, "You been to the house?"

Ben Tatum grunted in the affirmative.

Sam Wilburn worked in silence for a time, evidently doing a thorough job of it. The coarse brown hair fell on the apron in chunk's. Scattered among the brown, there were hairs that looked like copper wires, and there were more of them in his beard, especially on his chin. Those dark reddish copper hairs gleamed in his hair and short beard.

"What do you plan to do, now that the war's over?" Wilburn asked, his attention on his work.

"I ain't decided yet."

"You can't stay around here. They'll be looking for you."

Ben Tatum sighed, but said nothing. He sighed because he knew Sam Wilburn did not want him to stay around here. He had known already that they would be looking for him.

"Texas," Sam Wilburn said. "That's your best bet. I've been thinking about going down there myself. I don't think I'll like it much around here when the carpetbaggers move in. I don't like nobody telling me what to do or how to run my business."

"I doubt if it will be much better in Texas."

"Can't be any worse. Quite a few others around here and Hayville feel the same way. They've been talking about getting up a whole wagon train and going down there."

"I imagine talk about it is about all they'll ever do."

"No, they're serious. Even old Gip Snyder is talking about going. He says it's a new country with a lot of opportunities and we can build ourselves a new town down there where nobody won't bother us. Course, he plans to start a new bank, and I could start a new barbershop. The more I think about it, the better I like the idea."

"There'll be carpetbaggers in Texas just like there are here," Ben Tatum said.

"It won't be as bad. This state's been torn apart worse by the war than any other state in the country, and now that it's safe the carpetbaggers will be flocking in like vultures to pick our bones. Our money's already worthless. That's why old Gip Snyder is so keen on going. His bank at Hayville is in trouble, and he wants to salvage what he can and get out."

Ben Tatum shifted uncomfortably in the chair. "What about all the property he owns around Hayville?"

"I think he's found a buyer for most of it. That's the only thing that worries me. I don't know what I'd do with our property here if I went, and Cora ain't too keen on going. She's been in bad health lately. Losing them boys nearly killed her."

Ben Tatum was silent.

After a moment Wilburn asked, "What about the beard?"

"Get rid of it, I guess. Aunt Cora don't seem to like it."

After supper Ben Tatum went for a walk down along the creek. A path led him past an old shack almost hidden in the trees and brush. There was a light burning in the shack and through the window he caught a glimpse of a very shapely, blond-haired woman taking a bath. The long hair looked familiar.

When he got back to the Wilburn house he found Kittie in his room. "What are you doing here?" he asked, taking off the coat Aunt Cora had given him. It had belonged to Dave Medlow but it fitted Ben Tatum all right.

Kittie's lips curled back from her white teeth in a teasing smile. "Straightening up your room, Cousin Ben," she said with a deliberately exaggerated southern drawl.

"You run along," he said. "I'm not your cousin and the room don't need straightening up."

"That's right, we ain't cousins, are we?" she said. "We ain't no kin a'tall, now I think about it. But I was gonna marry you anyway. You sure do look handsome without that old beard. It made you look like a old man of about thirty."

"I'll be thirty before you're dry behind the ears," he said. He hung the coat in the closet and put his gun in a bureau drawer. In the mirror he saw Kittie Wilburn watching him with a smile, and he turned around with a frown. "Are you still here?"

"No, I'm still leaving. I just ain't got very far yet." She lay down on the bed and put her bare feet up on the gray wallpaper, so that her skirt fell down around her thighs, revealing very shapely legs for a skinny, thirteen-year-old girl. "Did you go see Rose?" she asked.

"Who?"

"Rose Harper. That girl who lives down by the creek. She just got back from Hayville a little while ago. I saw her go by. She lives over here now. Ever since she married Joe Harper. But she don't stay here much, 'cause he ain't never around. The bluebellies and nearly everybody else is looking for him, 'cause he rode with Quantrill. Like you."

"What does she look like?"

"Don't you know? You went to see her, didn't you? Anyway, you used to know her when she lived at Hayville with her folks."

"Wait a minute," Ben Tatum said. "Didn't Joe Harper marry that Hickey girl? Rose Hickey?"

"He shore did, Cousin Ben. He shore did."

"I thought that was what he told me after he came home the last time. My God, she was just a kid the last time I saw her."

"She ain't no kid now."

"She sure ain't," Ben Tatum agreed. "I saw her in Hayville and didn't even recognize her."

"I hate her," Kittie Wilburn said. "She makes me look plumb scrawny." She pulled her skirt up a little higher and looked at her thighs. "Do you think I'll ever outgrow it, Cousin Ben? Looking so scrawny and all?"

"You might," he said, "if I don't get mad and wring your neck."

"Oh, all right. I'll go." She swung her bare feet to the floor and rose, stretching and making a sort of groaning sound in her throat. She looked at him with that teasing smile. "But you've got to promise me something first."

"What?"

"I'll have to whisper it. I don't want anyone else to hear." She put her arms around his neck and rose on tiptoes, putting her warm moist lips close to his ear and whispering, "You've got to promise to marry me someday. Then I'll go."

"That'll be the day!"

She giggled and again made as if to whisper something, but this time she bit his ear and then ran from the room. At the door she pulled her skirt up to her waist, bent over and showed him her bottom. And it was quite a bottom for a skinny, thirteen-year-old girl to be flashing. He saw it in his mind until he went to sleep, and he wondered if he was the only one who had seen it. If so, it was probably only because she had not had an opportunity to show it to anyone else.

He knew he should tell Aunt Cora about the girl's naughty behavior, for her own good. But he also knew that he wouldn't, for his own good. Aunt Cora might think he had encouraged the child in some way, and think less of him because of it.

He slept late the next morning, and was awakened by the slamming of the door when Sam Wilburn left for the barbershop. He had just gotten dressed when he heard a dozen or more horsemen crowding into the yard, ordering all those inside to come out with their hands in the air.

http://amzn.to/1eDt8Fi

Son of a Gunfighter
http://amzn.to/17QAzSp

The Antrim Guns
http://amzn.to/132I7jr

The Bounty Hunters
http://amzn.to/10gJQ6C

The Bushwhackers
http://amzn.to/13ln4JO

The Fortune Hunters
http://amzn.to/11i3VsO

The Gundowners
(formerly So, Long Stranger)
http://amzn.to/16cOI2J

The Gundown Trail
http://amzn.to/1g1jDNs

The Hellbound Man
http://amzn.to/1fTATJy

The Hell Riders
Coming Soon!

The Last of the Fighting Farrells
http://amzn.to/Z6AyVI

The Long Trail
http://amzn.to/137P9c8

The Man Called Bowdry
http://amzn.to/14LjpJa

The Return of Frank Graben
http://amzn.to/1eeiDpk

The Revenge of Sam Graben
http://amzn.to/1c9lT7s

The Stranger From Hell
http://amzn.to/12qVVqd

The Vultures
http://amzn.to/12bjeGl

Wild Country
http://amzn.to/147xUDq

Wild Desert Rose
http://amzn.to/XH7Y27

About the Author:

Van Holt wrote his first western when he was in high school and sent it to a literary agent, who soon returned it, saying it was too long but he would try to sell it if Holt would cut out 16,000 words. Young Holt couldn't bear to cut out any of his perfect western, so he threw it away and started writing another one.

A draft notice interrupted his plans to become the next Zane Grey or Louis L'Amour. A tour of duty as an MP stationed in South Korea was pretty much the usual MP stuff except for the time he nabbed a North Korean spy and had to talk the dimwitted desk sergeant out of letting the guy go. A briefcase stuffed with drawings of U.S. aircraft and the like only caused the overstuffed lifer behind the counter to rub his fat face, blink his bewildered eyes, and start eating a big candy bar to console himself. Imagine Van Holt's surprise a few days later when he heard that same dumb sergeant telling a group of new admirers how he himself had caught the famous spy one day when he was on his way to the mess hall.

Holt says there hasn't been too much excitement since he got out of the army, unless you count the time he was attacked by two mean young punks and shot one of them in the big toe. Holt believes what we need is punk control, not gun control.

After traveling all over the West and Southwest in an aging Pontiac, Van Holt got tired of traveling the day he rolled into Tucson and he has been there ever since, still dreaming of becoming the next Zane Grey or Louis L'Amour when he grows up. Or maybe the next great mystery writer. He likes to write mysteries when he's not too busy writing westerns or eating Twinkies.

WARNING: Reading a Van Holt western may make you want to get on a horse and hunt some bad guys down in the Old West. Of course, the easiest and most enjoyable way to do it is vicariously – by reading another Van Holt western.

Van Holt writes westerns the way they were meant to be written.

Printed in Great Britain
by Amazon.co.uk, Ltd.,
Marston Gate.